Unlovable

Praise for *Unlovable*

Byron Jamal will be the breakout author this year. He has written a book that will make the reader take a look at his or her feelings about love, relationships, sexuality, and faith. I recommend this book as a must-read for everybody who wants to be a part of the healing of people and not the destruction of the human spirit.

J.L. King
New York Times Best-Selling Author

This work illustrates a fantastic personification of the beautiful diversity of life and love alike. The book, itself, is an extension of love that causes us to identify our most uncomfortable secrets of deed and thought. *Unlovable* makes obvious our fears and dreams that are within our grasp to be actualized so that hate is unsheltered and love is all we know.

Devin Michael
Artist and Father

Masterfully written, this book is a work that if we look closely, we will be able to find ourselves within its pages. Byron Jamal boldly shines a light into the hidden places of our heart and challenges how we love and who we love.

Pastor Anthony Roberts
Higher Living Christian Center, Dallas, Texas

Unlovable is a literary gift to those who have experienced the pain of societal or institutional rejection. Three broken and dark lives are woven into a colorful tapestry of love and affirmation. Byron Jamal has given a fresh clarion voice to the topics of sexuality, abuse, and hate, too often silenced when brought into dialogue with each other. This book will change you as much as it encourages you to believe in love again.

Dr. Tyrone Jackson
Human Resources Director, Washington, D.C.

Unlovable

FINDING LOVE IN THE MIDST OF THE UNLOVABLE

BYRON JAMAL

Byron Jamal

Visit my website at www.ByronJamal.com.

Printed in the United States of America

First Printing: November 2019
48Hour Books

ISBN- 978-1-7340412-0-0

For those who inspire and empower me to write as I do now:

Alain Locke (b.1885), Claude McKay (b.1889),

Langston Hughes (b.1902), Wallace Thurman (b.1902),

Countee Cullen (b.1903), Richard Bruce Nugent (b. 1906),

Bayard Rustin (b.1912), James Baldwin (b.1924),

Martin Luther King, Jr. (b.1929), Lorraine Hansberry (b. 1930),

Audre Lorde (b. 1934), Alice Walker (b. 1944),

Barbara Smith (b.1946), Octavia Butler, (b.1987),

Melvin Dixon (b.1950), Gloria Naylor (b.1950),

Joseph Beam (b.1954), E. Lynn Harris (b.1955),

James Earl Hardy (b.1966) and Janet Mock (1983).

Love is not just an action or feeling; it is an entity, a presence yearning for expression. Love is God, for God is Love.

—BYRON JAMAL

Contents

FOREWORD

Unlovable is a masterfully crafted drama bringing to the forefront secluded social issues that demand acknowledgment and penetrates the essence of reality. The theme of redemption and love provides an epiphany consisting of human struggles with dysfunctional behavior and societal norms but regenerates hope and compels compassion.

Be prepared to be pushed over the top of your comfort zone as the characters expose their unexpected flaws. Oliver is an alcoholic pastor with severe relationship issues. Rachel is First Lady of the church and pillar of strength but is gradually chipped away to almost nothing. Gloria is a single mom stripping to survive and support her daughter. While Brayden, an athlete dealing with his sexuality, is discovering an environment of discrimination and violence.

You can easily visualize what's happening with the dramatic reactions of each character outlined in an unhindered narrative. The combination of E. Lynn Harris, Zane, and Carl Weber; this author presents more than an old story in urban Christianity but thought-provoking concerns of present events. The reading of a faith-related book mixed with fiction uproots conflict and emotional appeal that touches various lifestyles, enlightening a message inside of the message.

This book invites you to explore the world of *Unlovable,* supplying vivid imagery of the "sinner" ministering to the "saint." The author teaches what we (the reader) need to learn: how to love unconditionally.

No matter what you may think about pastoral infidelity, hypocrisy, abuse, and dysfunctional heterosexual and LGBTQ relationships, you will always remember *Unlovable.*

"I may not think your actions deserve my acceptance, but your humanity demands it."

Kudos to Byron Jamal. You have created in life's journey a rhythm that is redefined in love.

The Call Path Review Team

Chapter 1: Oliver Clark, Jr.

First Sunday

∞ ∞ ∞

The pastor died today.

I know I don't belong here. This worn leather chair is uncomfortable. My knees don't fit under the old, oak desk. The swarthy brown wall color makes me nauseous. I cannot do this.

I feel a cold, clammy sweat forming on my palms. I decide to relocate to one of the many chairs of less distinction, a smaller one on the opposite side of the desk. It's where I spent so many days sitting. Just as I take my first step towards the chair, my eyes flash a glance at the portrait of the dead man. I freeze. The cold that embraced my hand now plagues my entire body. It's as if my system is experiencing a power outage, and only my eyes have a backup generator.

My eyes fixate on his broad chin. I recall days of gazing up at it. Fascinated, I would imagine it was a mountain ready to be climbed, but I rarely got close enough to touch his hand, let alone his face.

Those lips are plastered in the same position as they always were—a smirk. It was the same expression all the time, but somehow, I knew what emotion the dead man was attempting to convey. When those lips opened, they revealed a dark gorge where contradictory statements flowed. His jaded heart would speak love from the pulpit and hate at home. He abused me in ways that have left deeper scars than I care to uncover. What he failed to do with his massive, olive-skinned hands he accomplished with the refuse that spewed from his salmon pink lips.

The part of my brain that controls my inhibitions must be shut down as well because I shift up towards his eyes. I recount the first time the pastor ever slapped me. I was seven. I looked up at him in his eyes and shouted, "No!" It was like a solar eclipse. His hand brought darkness to my bright world. The vibrations of his hand against my left cheek left me temporarily deaf. I fell so hard and fast to the ground I could have been dropped from a twenty-story building with a boulder around my neck.

Much of what happened before and after is a muddled blur. I heard my terrified voice and the sound of his abrasive hand scolding my tender face. My body spins like a dreidel, falling with a distinct thud and corresponding moan and sigh. His pastoral tenor voice became a monstrous bass: "Don't EVER look at me in my eyes again."

Nothing is coming from his lips now. The portrait is contained in a half-inch of glass, held by a gold plated border. The words at the bottom read: "From the Church Family of Greater Mount Pleasant Baptist Church; In Honor of You, Pastor Oliver R. Clark, Sr." Even if he had a voice, no one could hear him now. I only hear my heart pounding and me panting. Even in death, he still affects me. My eyes lock to his like opposite ends of a magnet. They succumb to the same frozen state as the rest of my body. His eyes are ice shards piercing my bitter soul with incomparable accuracy.

It hurts to move. It hurts to breathe.

A heat begins to rise in me—emanating from the passion of my pain. My polar capped limbs start to thaw. My left hand, found resting on the dead man's desk, is freed first. My fingers crawl towards the edge and meet the snow globe created in honor of the first church dedication. Inside is a small replica of the original church building over forty-nine years ago. The decoration is as big as my fist and weighs as much as a healthy Chihuahua.

The sweat of my hand causes it to slide to the top of the glass globe. Before I can take another sharp breath, the enclosed world is out of my hand, soaring towards the dead man. I hear the water sloshing around just before the church replica smacks the pastor in the face. All the glass shatters. The snow globe's water soaks both the portrait and wooden floors.

I smirk.

The office door opens. It's my assistant, Shaw. "Is everything ok?" he inquires before seeing the wet and glass-covered murder scene to his left.

I wait, watching as Shaw's eyes pan to the left and head follows. As his jaw drops, he takes another step into the office and turns to face the portrait. Soon he forgets all about me. He's too busy staring at the wet dead man on the wall.

"What happened?" he asks, breaking his silence. He's a young Pre-Law major, so I know he can deduce that the globe didn't just launch itself towards the portrait. He's only asking out of obligation. Maybe deep in his heart, he is hoping the answer won't be obvious. He's not looking at me. It's visible he's nervous about my response.

As I take a step backward, I can feel the seat of the uncomfortable leather chair against the back of my leg. I take a deep, pain-free breath and fall back while exhaling. I situate myself in the chair, clear my throat and respond: "My father was thirsty."

Shaw adjusts his fashionably striped, rimless eyeglasses as his countenance scrunches in confusion and concern. He looks at me as if he is either waiting for me to laugh, confirming it was a joke or trying to remember where the yellow pages are so he can call a psychiatrist.

I smirk again. Shaw's face loosens.

"How about we get this cleaned up?" I propose, knowing Shaw would have stood there staring at me the rest of the evening if I didn't say something.

"Yes, sir." His lip is quivering as he backs out of the room.

I can hear it now: "Breaking News! A pastor is placed in a straightjacket and brought to Happier Times Mental Institution after suffering a psychotic fit due to the loss of his father." What a week. My bastard father dies, I give the best sermon of my life, and now I'm about to face charges of portrait manslaughter. Can it get any better?

"Pastor, I heard the noise. Is everything ok?" Deacon Archie DuBois asks as he pokes his lumpy, jet black, bald head through the cracked door. Looks like my day just got better.

"Deacon DuBois, I assure you everything is just—"

He gasps so hard he strips the oxygen from the air in the room. "What in the hell happened to Pastor Clark's portrait? What did you do?"

Oh, this day is shaping up nicely. "Deacon...there is no reason to use such language in God's house. We experienced a minor technical difficulty. It's nothing that a broom and mop can't resolve."

"Minor?" He scurries in front of the dead man, stepping on the glass as if it were supposed to be there. "You call this minor?" He stares at the portrait a moment. His right hand traces the wet canvas until it discovers a tear in the fabric. "My Pastor just died this week, and you are already desecrating his things. Your name should have been Cain. Your father—"

"My father is dead." My hands are gripping the arms of the chair so firmly that they are shaking. Sweat begins to appear on my brow. "I have been sworn in as Pastor of this church for almost five years. By now you should be used to that."

"Look, son. Don't you know why your father let you be the pastor?" As he pauses, his face contorts. The dead man's sinister smirk appears on Deacon DuBois' face. "Your father let you hold this office because he knew his health was failing and attendance was falling off. He needed fresh meat. Why do you think he came to all of your meetings? You only had two things he wanted: a fresh face and his name. You were like a puppy dog to a bone, playing his game."

I spring forward in the chair, with my elbows digging into the desk. "This is one mutt whose bite is worse than his bark. I would suggest you remove yourself from my office."

"Boy, you don't have any power here. Your threats don't move me."

"Well, I can assure you Deacon Archie Dean DuBois that I have other means than threats to move you." He folds his arms in defiance. "My dead father, your former pastor, showed me a trick on how to deal with your kind." I reach in the top drawer of my desk and grab a small white packet. I toss it at his feet.

His eyes follow the packet to the floor. "Salt?"

"Yeah. From what that dead man taught me, slugs can't stand the stuff. Now slither on back to your pit." My obdurate glare leaves him speechless. His smirk vanishes. His tongue is pressing against the back of his teeth so hard it appears he is about to growl. He is processing that I did not concede to his offensive language. Where did I discover this strength? After all of these years of allowing him to speak to me like some circus animal, I finally open my mouth and take a stand.

Just before Deacon DuBois grinds his teeth to dust, the office door creaks open.

"Dad...?" My ten-year-old son dashes into the office. He takes the silence as his cue to commence conversing with me. "Dad, where are we eating? Are you ready to go? I'm so hungry."

"Oli..." Even though he positions himself by my side, my eyes stay locked on Deacon DuBois. "The word is 'hungry.' Besides, can't you see I'm in the middle of a conversation with the good Deacon. It is rude to interrupt a conversation."

"But, Dad, you're not even saying anything. You're just looking at each other funny." This child is undeniably mine.

"Here's a teachable moment, son. You can learn a great deal about people by their actions." Without turning my head, I stand up and situate my hand on his shoulder. My wife appears in the doorway. "In fact, in most cases, what a person does can give you more insight into their true feelings than what they say. For instance, let's evaluate Deacon DuBois. How would you describe what his body is saying?"

I am barely able to finish the question before my son is attempting to answer. "Well, he looks like—"

"Okay...I found a broom and a mop," a voice says from behind my wife's body. As she steps to the side, Shaw appears. His crimson red shirt looks black from the sweat that is creeping through his pores. "I'm so sorry it took so long. The janitor left the broom in the choir stand and the mop in the bathroom downstairs. I've been running around trying to find them."

"It's quite alright." With so many witnesses in the room, I conclude my stare down with Deacon DuBois and face Shaw. "Just be careful with that glass."

In his youthful zeal, my son never examined the room upon entry. His curiosity temporarily overrides his hunger. He turns. "What happened to Grandpa's picture?"

"Nothing a mop and broom can't fix," Shaw says, busy trying to pick up the glass fragments. He looks up at me and nods. I guess while he was running around the church, he deduced why I was led to such an emotional response when I saw my father's portrait. He's worked with me long enough to know I am not crazy. Well, not that crazy.

"Indeed," I say, nodding back. Shaw returns his focus to the glass. "Rachel, dear?"

"Yes?"

My wife possesses the sweetest voice. Whether she is singing or having pillow talk with me in bed, her voice is soothing. She gets mad when I smile at her during arguments, but even when her voice is attempting to be angry, there's a beauty to it.

"Aren't you going to speak to Deacon DuBois before he leaves?"

She knows me better than anyone in this office. The tense energy I'm emitting does not go unnoticed by her. She must have seen the portrait, but she trusts me. Without any reservations, she proceeds to step to Deacon DuBois. He seems to cringe at her willingness to follow my lead. He releases a giant sigh and turns towards her. "Good day, Mrs. Clark."

"Have a wonderful evening, Deacon DuBois." I smile when I hear her again.

Deacon DuBois advances towards the open doorway. As he crosses over the threshold, he suspends movement. His head turns to the right. "We will be speaking with you soon, Pastor Clark." His hard-soled shoes amplify the sound of his footsteps as he marches away from the office door.

We all stand there in silence, waiting until the footsteps are only heard in our memories.

"Mom, I'm hungry." My son's persistence neutralizes the reticence in the room. I can't help but chuckle. Rachel's countenance lightens, and she laughs gently.

"Oli, what would you like to eat?" I already know what he is going to say, but I amuse him anyway.

"Let's get pizza."

No surprise there. Ever since Oli ate pizza at his ninth birthday party, he has wanted it almost every day after that. Maybe I have Italian in my family. I could sure use some "protection" right about now.

I look at Rachel. "Honey?"

"Yes, Pastor Clark?" She tries to say this seriously, but we laugh again.

"Do you think you have any Italian on your side of the family?"

§§§§§

The next morning, I awaken to the rumble of Oli's video game. I am sure it's the game where he's blowing up everything. My head feels like it has been through an explosion. I try to stand up out of my study chair, but end up falling to the floor with my arms flailing like a newborn.

Where's the trash can?

My vision is blurred, but the side of my face is familiar with this part of my study floor. I used to keep my trash receptacle across the room. After enough crawling sessions, I decided to keep it on the side of my cherry wood desk.

I crawl for what seems like an eternity. My hand lands on top of the tie that still hangs loosely around my neck. The vibrations of the game through the wood floors are making my stomach even more nauseous. I reach out my arm and grab hold of the edge of the metal container. At this point, sitting up is not an option. So I pull the can down and plunge my head inside.

It's never a pretty sight. That's why I lock my study door whenever I come in here. No one needs to see me in this state.

An hour passes, and I reawaken to a knock at the door. "Dad." It's Oli. Of course, it's Oli. My wife never disturbs me when I shut my study door. He's banging on the door and calling out my name. I love him so much. Words begin to form in my mouth, but there is not enough strength in my body to push them out. I moan. He can't hear me. I hear Rachel's voice.

"Dad's in his study. I'm sure he will be out soon." She said that so I could hear it. I lucked up when I married her. She is elegant and gorgeous, intelligent and witty, and understanding. Most of all, …she loves me. I'm afraid if she saw me in this condition, understanding and love wouldn't be enough to hold us together. My head is in my trash can, and it appears that I just slept in what I released in here.

Disgusted, I pull my head out of the receptacle. I jump to my feet, forgetting I still have a hangover. I'm too repulsed to be dizzy. I place the clean side of my face against the study door to hear if anyone is near. I only hear the video game. I unlock the door and sprint to the bathroom on the other side of the hallway. The toilet flushes. Nervous that Rachel might see me in my grey suit from yesterday with vomit on my face, I open the linen closet door beside the bathroom. I grab a towel, dash back into the study, and lock the door.

On my desk, I see the liquid culprit that has violated me. With every explosion of my son's game, it shakes, creating violent and then gentle ripples. That's about how my stomach felt an hour ago. I press the towel on my face, removing all the remnants of my indiscretion.

I've got to remove that bottle from out of this house. This is the last time.

I say that every time, but maybe this time will be different. Wrapping the damp towel around the bottle, I open my study window and climb out. My wife always wanted to know why I kept the bushes trimmed with space between the opening of the window. I walk between the bushes and find the large garbage bin on the side of the house. Tossing my package in the bin, I make my way back to the window. I realize the mail has arrived. I dart to the mailbox and run again with the speed of a greyhound.

Once inside, I shut and lock the window. There are mostly bills, but there is a small brown package addressed to me. The return address reads: From G.

I should have kept the bottle. I might need it depending on the contents of this package.

I rip the packaging open like it is Christmas Day. It's lined with bubble wrapping. My mother used to give it to me, and I would be popping away for a solid hour. But, right now, my concern is far from popping these bubbles. I turn the package upside down. A book falls out.

"A book?"

A small card is sticking out with something handwritten on it. It reads: *Read this book with care. It will help you love.*

"Help me with love?" I close the book and toss it on the desk. I'm just fine with love. I am going to go shower right now to remove this vomit smell so I can love my wife and son.

§§§§§

CHAPTER 2: GLORIA SANCHEZ

A Day in the Life

∞ ∞ ∞

I love this car.

It's the first one I ever bought with my own money. Men always want me to drive their cars. That's how this game works. I give the men what they want, and they just can't help but give me what they have.

I used to drive their luxurious, sporty cars, but not anymore. Not since my daughter began asking whose car we were going to drive that day. I remember driving Mr. B's new black BMW for about two weeks. Nahlia asked me to come to her school's Parent Day—where the parents spend part of the school day with their children. I was happy to be there with her. I just hated knowing I would have to stand in front of all those children and lie about what I do for a living.

When I pulled up, Nahlia's teacher saw me and walked over. "Good Morning, Mrs. Sanchez."

"It's Miss—" I lift my hand so she can see my naked ring finger. "But, good morning to you too, Mrs. Allen."

"Thank you, Miss Sanchez. I apologize for that. You just have such an expensive car. You must have a wonderful job to afford this, your stunning jewelry and outfits…"

That sandy blonde heifer was getting on my nerves. She was there every day I picked my daughter up from her elementary school. She knew I changed cars as often as my stilettos. I knew what she was trying to say. I would normally cuss her nosey ass out, but this was my daughter's school. I bit my tongue so hard that I thought I could taste blood. "It works for me," was all I can squeeze through my tight lips.

"Wonderful. Well, I can't wait to hear more about it when it's time for parents to present."

What she didn't know was that I was already preparing to have stomach cramps. I was at school, after all. When I was in school, I used to go to the nurse's office all the time with fake illnesses so I could get sent home. It always worked then, and it worked that day. I had Mrs. Allen feeling so bad that she wanted to pray with me. I'd become a pretty good actress. Nine years of doing this job, …it was only a matter of time.

When I left school that day, I turned the corner. I noticed an old, red Chevy truck sitting in someone's yard. There was a "For Sale" sign in the dash. I slowed down. It was like something was drawing me towards this truck. I pulled in the gravel driveway. I parked my BMW beside the truck and got out of the car. Dogs were barking in the distance as I walked up to the truck's passenger window and looked in.

"She's been through a lot." I'm startled by a voice that sounds like it should be singing "Sweet Home Alabama." He saw me nearly jump out of my Prada pumps. "Didn't mean to scare you there, Miss."

"Well, you did! You don't just walk up behind people like that. Where did you come from anyway?"

"Ma'am, I live here." He pointed to the small shed near a tall oak tree. "I was right on the otha' side of da' shed. You can't see 'er, but there is a small path through da' brush that leads to a field of flowers. Would'ja like to see?"

"Sir, look. It's nothing personal, but I don't know you. Plus, these pumps ain't cheap. I'm not just traipsing through anybody's field in these. If I want flowers, I'll buy them."

"Well, you're a feisty little thing," he says, extending his hand. "My name is Dale. Pleased to meet your acquaintance."

This grey-haired, white man was like all the other Mr.'s I've met. I just batted my lashes really good and let their wandering eyes do the rest. "Dale—" My seductive voice never fails. "What a strong name." He doesn't blink. As I began to move closer, I laid my hand on his arm. "I can tell you know how to—"

"Ma'am." He grabbed my hand. "You're a purdy lady and all, but if my wife saw ya touching on me like dat she'd have you tarred and feathered. They'd have to cut ya open to get those fancy shoes out yer behind."

I didn't know whether to laugh or cry. There has never been a man I couldn't conquer. If that fat S.O.B. wanted to keep hugging on that old piece of cornbread in his bedroom that was fine with me. No. It wasn't fine. My flawless victories over every man I've wooed have only proven that men are worthless dogs. This fatback eating lumberjack was messing with my head.

"It sure is hot out here." I was in full actress mode now.

"Lady, are ya interested in buying this car because I'm not interested in buying you."

"What?" I wanted to slap his Santa Claus cheeks, but I knew I was only mad because he was rejecting me. "Keep your old beat up hick mobile." Embarrassment pulled me towards the BMW. I fumbled with the keys until I found the unlock button. *Chirp!* I liked the way that car sounded when it opened itself to me.

"That's not yer car is it?"

"Why you say that?"

"I used to sell cars. I can spot it. Plus, a FOR SALE sign on an old truck actually made ya pull over." I just looked towards the road. "Look, I'm sorry for being a bit of a mule there. Ya just remind me so much of my youngest daughter, Emma. You'd like her. She's sassy too."

"If she is, we probably wouldn't get along too well." He even laughed like Santa Claus.

"Ya just might be right. Look, do ya want the truck?"

"How much is it?"

"Ya don't like answering questions straight much do ya?" He looked at me and shook his head. "How much do ya have?"

"Two thousand dollars."

"Sold. She's yers if ya want her."

"Wait; what?" I just started crying like I did when I found out I was pregnant with Nahlia. The same joy and fear came over me. I was happy that I was entering a new chapter in my life, but I was afraid I didn't deserve it and might mishandle it. I'd never owned something of my own. Even my daughter is only half mine. The other half belongs to a stranger.

He walked up beside me and patted me on the back in an attempt to console me. "There, there, dear."

"I'll take it," I say, crying as I looked at my first vehicle. "I'll come back later and get it."

A year passes, and I'm still crying.

Knock, knock, knock! "Mom, open up," Nahlia shouts, as the clumps of rain against the metal car muffle her voice. I should have been trying to catch a nap, but instead, I'm sitting here daydreaming. I unlock the passenger door to the truck while wiping away my tears. She yanks the door open. "Mom, what's wrong with you?" She plops down in the seat. Her hair is wet from the showers that have littered this week. "I've been standing out in the rain for like five minutes. I'm soaked." Her hands grip the door's handle, and she slams the door.

"Nahlia, baby, I'm so sorry. I must have dozed off." I am always sincere with my daughter. "But, unless you have money to replace a door or door handle on this truck, I suggest you save the drama for somebody who didn't carry you for nine months. Got me?"

"It's ok mom. I'm just ready to get home. School sucked today."

While she talks, I can't help but think about the fact that she has never once said anything bad about the truck. After all the luxury cars her friends saw her get into after school, she never complained when she found out I bought the bright red—slightly rusted—Chevy. In fact, she looked at me and smiled. The day I bought it, we celebrated the rest of the night with horror movies, greasy pizza, and butter pecan ice cream.

"Mom, are you listening to me." I don't know if it was her words or the aggravation in her tone that snapped me back into reality, but she had my full attention again.

"Huh? Don't take that tone with me, little lady. You become such a little diva when you get wet."

She points. I now realize that the horns blaring behind are for me. "Alright, I'm going," I say, shouting at the objects in the rearview mirror. "What do these people want from me?"

"The light's been green for a while. You just didn't go," Nahlia says.

Her words are more accurate than she knows. I wish life were that easy.

§§§§§

It's three hours until midnight. Leaving Nahlia is always the hardest part of this. Dropping her off at school is one thing, but leaving her home alone at night is something completely different. After I tuck her in bed, I kiss her on the forehead. Every night that kiss reminds me why I do this—so she won't have to.

I always end up standing in the long, silent hallway on the other side of the door, staring as if I could see through the brown metal door and into the darkness of my apartment. I never want to leave. It's as if sorrow waits for me at the door. There is no way to stop me from crying. You would think that years of doing this would have made my tears dry up, but they seem to flow harder.

I lock the two locks on the door and walk down the hallway with my small suitcase. After being here for nearly ten years, I still haven't gotten used to the pee smell coming from the walls where dogs and homeless people do their business.

As I press the "down" button on the elevator, my cell phone rings. "Somewhere Over the Rainbow" begins to fill the dimly lit hallway. It's embarrassing to cringe every time I hear a song that makes so many people smile.

He would kill me if he knew Pattie LaBelle was singing his ringtone. But he never hears it. Whenever he calls, he's waiting at the club for me.

"Hello, Stain." If I was standing in front of him, I know he would smell like cigars, malt liquor, and sex. Everything about him is rough. His words are harsh, his black, tattooed skin feels like sandpaper, and he sounds like he gargles with razor blades. It's just natural; my body tenses up when I talk to him.

The elevator door opens. I step on and turn towards the orange—yes, orange—painted walls. Maybe that color would look good in some fancy hotel or high rise, but here it's just awkward. It gives false hope. Some fools here think this is luxury. Maybe I'm the fool for being here. Nahlia would say that I'm stuck at a red light.

A young couple gets on the elevator and stands near the doors. They look like they're joined at the hip. As his hand gently rubs her shoulder, her hand slides down his back and rests in his back pocket. They must be newlyweds.

"Girl, don't you hear me talking to you? Where you at?" Stain's on the same b.s. like every other night. No matter how early I try to show up to the club, he's still complaining I'm late. "You have guys here waiting on you."

"I'm coming, Stain."

"You better watch that attitude little girl." Little girl? If he didn't look like an ax murderer out of a grainy 80's movie, I might have put my foot up his ass. "Hurry up. You're costing me money and making my client's unhappy." Here it goes. I can repeat this next part in my sleep. "If the clients are unhappy, then I'm unhappy; and, if I'm unhappy, then you're unhappy." I guess the clients are never happy because he makes my life a living hell.

The metal doors open. "Ok, Stain. I'll be there soon." I press the "end call" button hard like I'm slamming a phone down. It doesn't have the same effect but makes me feel just as good.

As the couple exits the elevator, the lady looks back to see what kind of woman talks to a guy named Stain. I snap my head forward, "Yes?" She grabs the guy's arm, pulling him away quickly. The elevator door almost closes. I put my arm out to catch it. The crisp near-midnight air is soothing to my overheated emotions. The short walk outside to my truck gives me time to say a short prayer for peace and safety. As I drive down the interstate, the wind from my open window erases the tears and prepares my heart to put on my alter ego again.

When I arrive at the club with the huge neon sign—Platinum Dolls—, I pull my rusty cherry red truck in front of the huge glass doors. The attendant opens my door. "Hey, Steve."

"Good evening, Elle." They only call you by your stage name here. He grabs my bag in the back seat and hands it to me as I walk past him. "Do well tonight." Steve has been here almost as long as I have. I guess we are work friends in passing. He's a cute little white guy.

"Honey—," I look over my shoulder knowing he's eating this up. "Elle Chanel can't be anything less than the best." I wink, turn and strut my Latin sass into the dingy brick building.

I walk up to the guard at the front. Since Stain told the guards at the front to never speak to the girls, this big mass of hardened marshmallows just points to the side door that leads down to the back of the stage. It's best to arrive at this time. I don't have to worry about changing with all the girls. By now, they are out on the floor getting their tips.

It never takes me long to change in an empty room. I pretend that Stain is standing behind me barking for me to take off my clothes. I change like Wonder Woman that way. A girl who just finished on stage comes through the curtain. "I think you're up next. You better hurry."

Hurry. This nurse uniform only takes 10 seconds to put on and half of that to take off. "Thanks," I say without looking at her. She crosses the room and sits at the mirrored desk next to her locker. None of the girls really talk here. Stain discourages it. He believes there is less drama when the women don't talk. He always likes to say: "There are less foul eggs when the chickens don't talk in the coup." Sometimes I think he sits around all day thinking of dumb sayings like that.

Stain also thinks eye contact is unnecessary. He tells us to pretend we are the only ones working. We come to dance on stage and work the clients then leave. He wants us to be less coworkers and more strangers—even if we become strangers to ourselves. If he could work it out, he would have us all completely separate. It's probably so we don't know he's messing with all the girls that work for him, even Isis—the married one who had the sores that everyone thought was herpes. Only the young naïve ones believe he actually loves them.

I used to be young and naïve. Now, I'm older and wiser. One good thing about the girls not talking is I don't have to hear the young ones calling me old. "I really am getting too old for this," I say, tying my thirty-year-old hips in a string bikini and jumping into a nursing outfit.

I hear my music begin. No one checks to see if I'm ready. It's assumed that I am. I better be. There are no valid excuses in this place.

"Coming up to the stage is Elle Chanel." The announcer always gives me the shortest intro because I won't sleep with him. Maybe if he didn't talk like a Latino hillbilly or dress like a homo clown, I might think about letting him walk me to my car at night. He just does nothing for me. And, for that, he introduces me like I just started at the club. There's no reason to complain. He makes every day feel like the first day all over again.

I step to the curtain. It's time to punch in. Another day, another dollar.

§§§§§

CHAPTER 3: BRAYDEN FOSTER

New Beginnings

∞ ∞ ∞

I'm scared.

Looking out the private plane's window, I can't help but think about all I'm leaving behind. Below are clouds that look like someone took bleach and splattered it across the landscape. Those clouds might as well be doing that with my life. I just left Beverly Hills, and it seems everything is being erased. My family, friends, even my Porsche are all left well over two thousand miles behind. I just keep trying to look through the whiteness of the sky to find a trace of life below—a car, house…something.

Suddenly, I feel a firm hand on my shoulder. "What time is it, Brayden?" I hadn't realized my father was awake again. Since he's so used to planes, he's typically knocked out when his skull hits the headrest.

"It's 5 p.m. Charlotte time, Dad."

"How do you feel? Just two more hours and we will be in Charlotte, North Carolina."

"It feels—" I don't know why I thought he was actually asking for my opinion. It was only hypothetical. Maybe I was staring into the clouds too long.

"Tomorrow you'll be in your dorm room at my alma mater. Isn't that exciting? Huh?" My mouth opens again. I must think he is somehow talking to me. "Good ole' Charlotte University…home of the Hornets."

It looks like he's just staring into the overhead light. I'm sensing a story about to come.

"Son, did I ever tell you about the time our basketball coach took us jogging in the woods and we got lost for two days?" I refuse to answer. "It was my sophomore year—"

His words are drowned out by my thoughts. I should be interested in the history lesson. My father believes in sharing his stories of becoming a black millionaire who started from nothing. He has dined with the Obamas, did "Dancing With the Stars," and been in boardrooms with the Trumps. I respect his hustle, but even the most exciting stories can get boring after hearing them several dozen times.

My father startles me with an assertive nudge. "Wake up, Brayden. We have arrived." I hate rolling my eyes at my father, but it feels instinctive. On our way off, Dad says, "Another excellent flight, Stan. I barely knew we were moving."

"Oh, Mr. Foster, that's what you pay me to do," the pilot, says.

"I guess you have a point there," Dad says. "If I could just get employees like you in my California office, I'd be worth another million." I can't tell whose laugh is drier, the pilot's or my father's.

If my father weren't a bank executive at the most significant international bank in the country, handling my luggage would've been the worst part of the trip. He hired movers to pack all of my possessions and bring them to the airport. When we arrived, the Charlotte-based movers were already there prepared to move my stuff off the plane, bringing it to our room at the Ballantyne Resort.

While my dad was telling the movers which bags were mine, I happened to see a tall, slim, middle-aged, black guy with a fitted cap holding a sign with my name on it. He sees me staring at him and points to the card and then me. I nod. As he walks over, I realize it's Coach Bridge. I couldn't recognize him at first. Maybe I did stare at those clouds too long.

"Hey, Coach."

"Well, hey there, champ. Did you have a good flight?"

"Yeah, it was cool. I was—" I was about to express an actual thought of my own with my father around. I don't know why I tried. I can't say anything with him near.

"Coach Bridge!" My father erupts with pleasure. I swear he almost giggles. "How are you?"

"I'm well, Mr. Foster. I just wanted to come and make sure you two got in alright."

"Why thank you, Coach."

"No problem. I also wanted to drop these off." He dangles a pair of keys in front of my father.

"What is it?" I ask with the curiosity of the five-year-old.

"These are the keys to your rental truck. I wanted to make sure you had more than enough room to move your items tomorrow. You can store them on here and take them off in the morning."

"Great idea, Coach Bridge," my dad says, already taking steps backward. "Let me go tell the movers about the change of plans." At fifty-years-old, he still sprints to the movers.

Coach turns to me. "I see where you get your intensity on the court."

What I want to say is that my dad is a super control freak, stressing over every little thing that doesn't go his way. I look at the coach and shake my head. "I can't take my father anywhere."

By the next day, my father is seizing command of every minute. If he could control my breaths and heartbeats, I'm pretty sure he would.

"Get up, Brayden!"

Not much makes me jump, but when I have a 6'3", two hundred pound man screaming in my ear when I'm sleeping, I can't guarantee anything. "Ah!" My body jumps so high in the air that it feels like I bounced on a trampoline. I fall off the bed on to the hardwood floors. As I land on my stomach, the wind in my lungs is forced out.

"Dad, what is wrong with you?" I'm gasping for air as if I nearly drowned.

"Get up, Brayden." Why does he sound like a drill sergeant? "We have a long day ahead of us. You need to get showered, shave, iron, and put on your clothes. Then, we need to—"

I'm too busy trying to get to my feet to go over his play-by-play of how the day should run. I moan as I balance myself. With my dad still talking, I gather my shower items and walk into the bathroom, shutting the door behind me. And, yes, he is still talking with the door closed. I yank my clothes off of my body and sit on top of the closed toilet seat. Reaching into the shower area, I turn on the hot water to create my own sauna. I bend over, placing my elbows on my knees and fingers in my ears to block the noise on the other side of the door.

There is so much I want to tell him. It is going to be a really long day.

§§§§§

We arrive on the campus of Charlotte University in the rental truck the coach provided. It is the happiest I've seen my father for a long time. He leans over to me and points. "We are here. Now, over there is the statue of Martin Luther King, Jr. that the student body and I worked to purchase. That's the Brice Arena where you will be spending a bulk of your time practicing. Over there is the tree where I first kissed your mother—God rest her soul." He almost frowned. "And, that's the Pierce Student Union. That's where you'll find all the girls." He makes sure to nudge me a little and raise his eyebrows.

We pull up to the dorm. Coach is waiting outside. He opens up my passenger door. "Good morning, Brayden. Good morning, Mr. Foster."

Dad and I sound like junior cadets. "Good morning, Coach."

"Well, are you ready to move in?"

I hesitated, half thinking he was asking hypothetically. He just kept staring at me. "Oh, yeah. I'm ready." Dad puts his hand on my shoulder before getting out of the truck. I know it means a lot that I'm going to his alma mater. I can't say I wanted to go here. It's one of the highest-ranked schools in both athletics and academics, but it's too far from home.

"Let's get you moved in, champ. Follow me." We trail the coach towards the mint green metal doors. He stops like he's stuck. "A few years ago, I implemented the rule that all junior and senior athletes must help one freshman teammate move in. It helps create a sense of family and ensure seniors stay connected with their incoming teammates." Coach peers through the glass as if he is expecting someone. "Where is that boy?" He must have seen the guy because he opens the door enough to poke his head through. "Jakes, come here and meet Foster and his father."

Through the metal double doors walks my first temptation in Charlotte—Jakes. He steps beside Coach Bridge and flashes a smile that could stop a horde of stampeding bulls. He's wearing an old Jersey that exposes his lightly tanned chiseled arms. I can tell he's mixed with something because his lips are full, but his hair looks smooth like mulberry silk.

I'm doing my best not to stare. I put my head down. Coach slaps Jakes on the shoulder, saying, "Don't be rude to Foster. Where are your manners? Introduce yourself." I know Jakes is about to step towards me, but my emotions are entirely unprepared to handle his presence.

"Hey," he says, as he extends his hand, "I'm Jakes Heart." The way I hold out my hand must make me look like an enamored fan seeing a celebrity crush in person. My tongue feels glued to the roof of my mouth. There's no way he is missing the discomfort in my face. He takes my hand and shakes it abruptly. It is firm and sharp, but his hand is still smooth and creamy. I'm so stunned that I can feel myself about to drool. "You're Brayden Foster. Good to meet you."

My eyes are like darts aimed everywhere but in his direction. With my heart racing and hands tingling, I swallow so hard I think my throat is closing. *Am I having an allergic reaction?* "Jakes," says Coach, "why don't you show Foster his room. He can make a game plan of how he wants us to position his items in there." The Coach maneuvers around Jakes to walk to my father.

"Come on, fresh meat. Let's check out your new room." Jakes and I walk through the green, wooden doors into the lobby. "What do you think, newbie? Nice…huh?"

As he looks back at me, I'm wiping my hands on my pants and clearing my throat. "Yeah, it's cool." The mid-size chandeliers, gold accents, and antique décor are more than cool. They're stunning. But, right now, the best thing I see is this sculpted mass of flesh in front of me.

I didn't even see him hit the button for the elevator, but I walk on behind him. "Hit '3.'" I press the button. We're alone, so if I want to talk now is the time. I clear my throat again. "Are you ok man? Do you have something going on in your throat?"

"No. No. I'm cool." I take a deep breath in and exhale. "So, how do you like school so far?"

"That's a typical freshman thing to ask." I'm staring at him confused as to why he's now laughing at my question. "Look, I love it here, but whether I like it or not won't change if you do. So, do you like it here?"

Ding. "We're here," I say, appreciating being saved by the elevator bell.

"Not quite. Follow me." I shadow his steps off the elevator and down the elegant corridor to my room—302. "Now, we're here." He opens the door.

"I have a suite?" I ask, walking into the spacious room.

"Yep. The only downside is you're next door to a band member, so you'll have to put up with them practicing."

"Wow! Who cares? This space is great," I say.

"Oh, it's great now? Are you sure it's not just cool?"

I'm getting some strange energy from him. Does he not like me? Did I do something to offend him? My eyes scroll down from his face and land on his arms again. His biceps look like small boulders wrapped in honey silk.

Focus Brayden.

"Hello! Are you there?" he asks.

"Huh?"

"I said that we should probably start moving your stuff in," he says. "If you're on some medication or something—"

"No, no, no." I realize that his Greek-god physique and modelesque beauty is making me act silly. *Pull it in Brayden.* "I'm joking man. Let me check these rooms out."

Jakes shrugs. "Okay, Foster. I'm just saying that if you do take anything—"

I punch him, playfully, in his shoulder. "Dude, I don't take anything. Can you guys take a joke at C.U.?" He laughs and shakes his head. I wonder what he's thinking. A few minutes in and I haven't made the best first impression in my room. What I need to be worried about is what everyone thinks of me on that court.

By the time I finish figuring out how I want to organize my spacious bedroom and bathroom, Dad and Coach have made it through the doorway. Coach says, "I have your stuff, Foster. Where are you?"

"Back here." My phone begins to vibrate. "Oh, God…" I start searching the room for my vibrating phone. Jakes stares at me like he knows I'm crazy.

"Foster, relax. You will find your phone. Just calm down."

That sounds simple enough, but at any second Maxwell's "Pretty Wings" will resound through my empty suite. I can't let Jakes, Coach, and my Dad hear that. Just as I realize it's on the bathroom sink, the tile gives acoustic support to the tunes that are now playing. I scramble to get to the phone and answer. "Hey, Brittany. How are you?"

"What took you so long to answer?" Is she starting already?

"I'm well. How are you?"

"What are you doing?" I know she cares, but Brittany is the type of L.A. girl who feels entitled to get whatever she wants. Right now, what she wants is me.

"Are you not even worried if I'm ok?"

"Of course, I am. You didn't call me last night like you said you would," she says, ignoring the text I sent last night telling her I wasn't up for talking and would call her today once I settled in. With Brittany, there's no point in bringing that up.

"My bad, Brit."

"Of course, it is. Do you miss me?"

"For sure."

"Aren't you nervous about us doing this long-distance relationship? I am. But, I wouldn't want to try it with anyone but you."

I poke my head around the corner. Jakes, who is now sharing my instructions to my Dad and Coach about where I want my stuff, looks at me and laughs. I'd laugh too if I heard my ringtone. The worst part is that I didn't even choose it. Brittany changed it one day when I left it at her house. I walk out of the bathroom, placing the phone against my chest. "I'm going downstairs to look at the rest of the stuff in the truck." I sprint out of the room and down the hallway. "Brittany, we need to talk."

"About what?

"This…us…our relationship."

"Brayden! We already talked about this relationship. We talked about it for like a month before you left. We fought about it, cried about it, and made up over it. What else is there to talk about?"

I still don't know who gets under my skin more, her or my father. My father approves of her because her family is almost as wealthy as us. She passes my father's "class" test. She is jaw-droppingly gorgeous with all the high school stats in her favor: head cheerleader, student council president, valedictorian, and prom queen. My dad would say that we are a perfect union.

"This won't work." She's silent for a moment. "Hello? Brittany, are you there?"

"Oh, I'm here. I was waiting for you to finish talking to whoever you were speaking to right there. I know that wasn't for me."

"It was."

"What? You're kidding me, right. You've only been there a day, and you are already trying to get rid of me? Did you meet someone else already?"

"Well, no, but—"

"I don't understand. Why are you doing this to me?"

"I'm not trying to do anything to you. You don't understand. It's not about you. This is about me."

"It's always about you, Brayden."

"No. It's not. I just…I…I just know this won't work." I'm not the type of person to stammer, but this isn't like anything I've dealt with before. Who turns down the perfect woman? Maybe this is just a phase, nervousness about such a big move?

"What won't work? It worked when I was there to massage you when you were sore from hours of practice. It worked when I was there calming you down when you were nervous about your championship game. It's worked from middle school to today. You were my first, and you can tell me you don't think it will work? You're just sorry!"

"I'm not trying to hurt you."

"Well, you did. You hurt me. You're selfish and inconsiderate. What is it then? What could break us up after all this time?"

"I'm gay." I blurt it out like a water hose with a leak in it.

"Be serious, Brayden. I've known you all this time. What is it? Be a man and tell me."

"I just did." The levees holding back my tear ducts breach, and my pain begins to stream down my red cheeks.

"Why didn't you tell me you were a faggot? You should have told me you liked men. So, you're cheating on me with men this whole time?"

Trying not to sound like I'm crying, I say, "I've never cheated on you, and I've never been with a man."

"Well, how do you know you like men then?"

"I just know. I feel it."

"So, I turned you to men?"

"No! I've known since I was little."

"Well, I was going to tell you to go to hell, but, if this is true, looks like you're already going. Forget my number." She hangs up.

I sit there a minute with my ear to the phone, listening to the dial tone. I thought this was going to be a memorable day, but this isn't how I expected things to go. Miles away from her unforgiving glares and ridicule, her words make me feel like she is standing right beside me.

By now, I'm outside standing at the back of the truck. I hear the double doors open. It's Dad and Coach. "Where's my son?" I move to the opposite side of the truck and crouch down.

"Maybe he's off getting acquainted with the school gym." They laugh as they pull more items off of the truck and take them up to my room.

Hell? I'd thought of hell before, but it's something about the way she said it. There was so much hurt and hatred in her voice. It's like she was putting the final judgment on my life. How could see damn me to hell?

I don't know how long I've been crying. But my dad is now standing over me. "Boy, what's wrong with you? I've been looking for you for almost an hour. Coach wants you to call him when you get settled. You have one more bin to move in. Here!" He extends his hand to help me up. As I stand, he sees the dampness of my shirt and redness in my eyes. "Have you been crying?" I don't respond. "What happened? You should be happy."

I never knew "happy" was my trigger word, but something in me snaps. "Well, I'm not happy!" In my eighteen years of life, I have never yelled at my father, but today is different.

"Here we are at one of the best schools in the nation. You have a full scholarship to play on the top team in the division. Look at where you're living. Brayden, how can you say you're not happy? What else do you need?"

"I don't know. I just want to be happy," I say.

"Son, I can get you to a shrink if you need one?"

"I don't need a shrink, Dad. I like guys."

He takes a step back as if I just struck him. "What?"

I never thought I could tell my dad like that. "I like guys. I always have. I just never did it."

"What does that mean?"

"I just told Brittany," I say, swallowing another lump in my throat. "We just broke up."

"You broke up with Brittany?" Dad pauses and stares at me. "Is this some kind of sick way of getting back at me for pushing you to come here?"

"No, Dad. I just—"

"I was tough on you growing up, but I didn't know you hated me this much." He throws his hands up and grunts. "I can't take this!"

"Dad…"

"Get out of my way," he says. "I can't even look at you."

He pushes past me and gets in the driver's side of the truck. As he slams the door, the car starts, and he backs out of the space without even looking.

"Dad!" I'm banging at his door, begging him to listen. I've never wanted him to stay around so bad. Through my screams, I can hear the car shift to "Drive." He takes off like a NASCAR racer. The last bin holding my clothes falls open as it crashes from off the back of the truck. I'm paralyzed. An open truck is speeding away from me with my clothes littered across the pavement like trash in Brooklyn.

Isn't this hell?

My crying resumes, but the weirdest of thoughts come to my mind. I'm glad it wasn't my T.V. I try to laugh; only more tears follow. Jakes charges past me, gathering up my clothes, placing them back in the bin. He picks it up and carries it to me.

"Where were you?" I ask.

"Dude, I live on the first floor. I saw your dad drive off. I'm supposed to look out for you." He puts his hand on my shoulder. "Let's get you up to your room. This isn't the best place for you to be crying."

It seems like the longest journey to my room. I can't see anything but the back of that truck pulling off down the street. When we reach my suite, he says, "You should go wash your face." Dazed, I meander to the bathroom and run some warm water, splashing a little on me. When I lift my head, I can't even look at myself in the mirror. The water hits my face a few more times. I turn the faucet off and realize I don't have a towel.

I look up in the mirror and see Jakes standing behind me with one of my towels in hand. "I thought you could use this." He throws it over my shoulder and walks back into the bedroom. I throw my face into the crimson red towel, holding it there long after my face is dry.

I'm smiling. I can't let Jakes see that. I think of the truck again. It works. My disposition drops in the towel.

I leave the towel on the sink and walk back into the bedroom. Jakes moved my bed near the window. "You seemed like you still needed fresh air. I hope you don't mind; I made the bed for you." He went in my bags, found my sheets, and made my bed. I guess God is giving me a little heaven after all the hell I just went through. "Just lay down. I'll check on you later."

"Okay."

He tucks me in. As I watch him walk out of the room, a lazy breeze cools the fresh tears rolling down my face.

§§§§§

CHAPTER 4: OLIVER CLARK, JR.

Coal-Colored Clothes

∞ ∞ ∞

There is a melancholy silence in the midnight black limousine.

Rachel, Gwen, Oli and I all peer through our respective tinted windows. I am sure each of us has a unique perspective on this silence. I view it as a way of not speaking ill of the dead. Rachel probably believes her silence is helping me cope with the loss of my beloved father. Oli's disinterest in talking stems from his hurt feelings when I bawled at him for playing around the gravesite.

"Oli, come sit here for a moment." I tap the seat lightly, directing him between Rachel and me. Somehow his right foot is snagged on his left, and he lands on his face in front of my feet.

"Well, now I see why the boy doesn't play sports," says Rachel's mother, Gwen. "He has his mother's coordination." Oli springs up and rests beside me.

"Mom!" I only see Rachel truly aggravated when her mother starts talking about her. "He just tripped." Rachel rubs Oli's head while staring at her mother.

"Just tripped," Gwen says as she turns to me. "Oliver did I ever tell you the time your just wife tripped at the ice rink?"

"No. I don't think so." I say, watching Rachel shake her head. She probably would've said something, but she wouldn't refuse me a good laugh on a day like today.

"She saw some of the other girls doing turns, so she decided she wanted to do one too. The problem was she barely knew how to skate in the first place. You should have seen her. She was like that starting domino that knocks all the others down. Oh, and down they all went. Little girl scouts, big biker guys and I think even a nun topped over in her whirlwind of chaos."

"A nun?" asks Oli, forgetting his crusade of silence.

"Honey, if your mom didn't tie her shoes sitting down, she'd fall right over." Oli looks up at his mother but decides against it when he sees her critical countenance.

When I observe his reaction, I wrap my arm around him. "Gwen, you're not going to frighten Oli today." I'm doing my best not to laugh. "He can do all things by faith."

"Child...," Gwen says, "he's going to really need some divine intervention if he has Rachel's balance. We better pray right now." Even Rachel, looking flushed, couldn't help but laugh.

§§§§§

There is a cavalcade of rolling metal following the limousine. As we park and exit the vehicle, I can see bodies arrayed in coal-colored clothes trailing us. I can barely open the house door before it is full of hungry mourners.

Just as I open the blinds, I see Deacon DuBois trekking across my lawn towards the front door. "Oh God," I say with all the joy of a priest on Halloween.

"Yes?" A deep voice with a massive limb snags my neck. "It is I. God. What do you want my son?"

"Terry, you nut job."

Terry gasps as I deliver one swift elbow to his side. "Hold up, preacher. You're not supposed to be hitting people like that."

"Not everyone was in the army like you. I'm just a soldier in the army of the Lord," I say still looking out the window. "I had my basic training before I got saved, so it was a bit more hands-on than normal."

"I don't know whether to call you Pope or Popeye. What are you looking at now?" He peers through the open blind and looks back at me, nodding.

"Right," I say, with my thumb pointing to the window. "He's here."

"Come on. Let's go in your study," Terry says, dragging me away from the window. After he slams my door, Terry tosses me into my study chair, as he has done so many times before. "You're getting soft in your old age, Junior. I'm going to have to send a shuttle to come get you."

"For what?"

"They'll pick you up to go play late-night bingo with the Silver Foxes senior group."

"Well, they would be picking you up too. You are only two years younger than me," I say, crossing my legs.

"What can I say? Thirty looks good on me," Terry says. "Speaking of old, how do you feel about the good Deacon being in your house?"

"Like this," I say as I reach in my drawer and pull out a new bottle of gin and two glasses. "Do you want a drink?"

"You're joking, right?" he asks, taking the bottle away.

"I just want to make a toast," I say, raising my empty glass above my head.

"Why is that bottle in here? You're not supposed to be drinking. What is the point of me being your sponsor if you're going to drink right in my face?"

"Terry, we just lost the pastor of Greater Mount Pleasant Baptist Church. I think that deserves a toast."

"You are the pastor of the church. Not him. Besides, you only toast over celebrations or—"

"That is my point exactly. We are toasting the death of the former pastor and the hopes that Deacon DuBois will be next."

"Junior, you can't toast to that," Terry says.

"Why not?" I ask, motioning for the gin.

"We've been friends since we wore diapers, and I've never heard you say something so mean and hateful." Terry places the gin on the edge of the desk closest to him and begins pacing. "Something's gotten into you. When was your last drink?"

Silence.

"Junior, when was your last drink?"

More silence.

"What is the point of being in A.A. if you can't answer that question?" I can see his concerned frustration mounting inside of him. "Answer me, goddamnit!" His fist sounds like a cinder block as it slams into my desk.

"You will not take the Lord's name in vain in this house," I snap.

"You want to get self-righteous? Fine! When was your last drink, pastor?" Terry folds his arms and stares at me. He knows that if we were playing chess, he just checkmated me.

"Sunday night."

"Junior, that's not right. You've been making progress for years now. Why are you doing this to yourself?"

I grab the bottle of gin. "I'm doing it for the same reason I'm about to drink now. I need it." I pour some into my glass and take my first sip of gin. "There's nothing wrong with celebrating the former pastor's homegoing. We did that at the funeral service."

"That's not the same, Junior. Everyone— except for you it seems—was happy that he went on to a better place. We just left a church packed with news organizations, CEOs, community leaders, and people whose lives he touched. You got to meet the President of the United States today, and you're sitting there trying to toast that he's gone. That's not even the same thing. I know you don't like Deacon DuBois. Hell, not many people do. But, you ought to know better than wish the man dead."

"Don't tell me what I wish, Terry," I say, thrusting my body out of the chair. "I can damn well wish for what I want." I pour another gulp of gin down my throat. "I wish a lot of things that don't happen. When I was growing up, I wished that Deacon DuBois would disappear and never return. It was around college when I began wishing he would die."

"Junior, you don't wish any such thing," Terry says as he stops pacing.

"I wished I had a father," I say, finishing the drink while falling back into the study chair.

"You have a father. You just buried him."

I pour another drink. "No, I had a pastor and a sperm donor. That's the only way I know him. He was never any more than that."

"Junior, calm down. Your father loved you. I know. I watched him while we were growing up. He took care of you and your mother. I saw that with my own two eyes."

"What you observed was the gaudy farce my father mastered. His love was as fake as the blood in a Hollywood movie."

"He's dead bro," Terry says. "Let him rest in peace."

"Peace? He doesn't deserve it. He never once brought my life a modicum of peace."

"I know you're hurting."

"You don't know anything. You're just—"

"I know you better shut the hell up and listen to me," Terry says, stretching his thick neck so that every vein in it bulged. "Long before he was your father, he was a human being. I hate to tell you what you already know, but maybe you need to hear it again. People hurt each other. We often pass the pain of our issues on to others, especially the ones we love."

"But, he was a Pastor," I say.

"And, so are you! Are you really going to tell me that you're perfect?"

"You're taking his side, Terry."

"He's dead. He doesn't have a side. The only thing on his side right now is a casket and dirt. Besides, I'm always on your side. Being a pastor, you know better than anyone that God forgives us with the same measure we forgive others."

"Stop trying to pull that pastor crap on me. Regardless of what I am, he was a horrible father. He never loved me." I slam my empty glass on the table. Terry snatches the gin bottle away before I can reach for it again.

"Alright! You're on some other stuff right now." He turns away from me and stares out the window. Silence invades and lingers in the room like a horde of hungry Vikings. "You know my cousin, Amir?" I've never heard Terry's voice quiver like this before.

"Isn't that your oldest cousin?"

"Yeah. Well, when I was young, he took advantage of me."

"What?" The shock in my voice was in part because he looks like Shaq and has never been without a woman.

"You heard me."

"I'm sorry."

"I don't want your pity," Terry says as he turns towards me with his eyes swelling with liquid sorrow. "I want you to listen to me." He redirects his focus back to the open window. "I felt like I couldn't tell anyone. After that day, everything was weird between us. When he saw me at family gatherings, he would go the other way. The older we got, the less I saw of him. Soon, he stopped coming to family events altogether. I thought I would always hate him. I could have, but I realized that those feelings were tearing me up inside. My bitterness towards him was creeping into other relationships too."

"How did you deal with it?"

"I buried it. And, well, you know this part. As soon as I got to college, I stayed drunk and high. I used every drink to numb the pain. I wasn't drinking for the moment; I was drinking for what happened in my past. What you don't know is that five years ago, I finally told my mother what happened. I just broke down, man. I couldn't even help it. I was twenty-five, a jock, and still crying like a baby. She just began to pray with me: God grant us the serenity to accept the things we cannot change, courage to change the things we can, and wisdom to know the difference. She had me repeat those words, and soon I was going to A.A meetings. That helped me come to a place where I could forgive him and deal with my alcohol issues. Then she told me something that sealed it for me."

"What did she say?"

"She told me that he was molested by his friend's father when he was a child." Terry walks over to me and sits where the gin used to be. "My hatred for my cousin was continuing the cycle of hate. Amir hated that man, but he took his hatred and did something evil—wicked—to me. He didn't hate me; he loved me. But, when people let their hurt grab hold of them like a snake bite that pain can act just like venom. It doesn't care who it affects. He let that hurt bite me, but I refuse to let my hurt cause anyone else pain. Junior, you be careful. I don't want you letting your hurt cause the ones you love pain. You have to love them enough to want to keep them safe—even if it's from you."

"Dad!" Oli yells from the other side of the study door. "Dad stop hiding. Mom wants you out here."

"Alright, son. Tell mom I am coming out momentarily."

"Junior, my friend. I'm praying for you. I know it's not easy with everything that you are feeling towards your father. But, you have to know that pain will come out one way or another if you don't deal with it. You know I'm here for you."

"I know you are. Thanks, Terry."

"They don't call me Terr-if-ic for nothing."

"Oh, please." I start laughing. I laugh until the pain the alcohol couldn't affect goes numb. I laugh until I don't even remember why I'm laughing.

"Look, bro," Terry says, looking at me like I have lost my mind. "There's one person I'm afraid of more than you."

"Who is that?"

"Rachel," Terry says, chuckling. "Let's get you out to her and the rest of your celebrity guests." I reach for his extended hand, and he pulls me out of the chair. "Are you ready?"

"As ready as a slightly inebriated pastor can be."

"On second thought, maybe you need to sit back down."

§§§§§

All the sympathizers for the dead pastor are gone. They left with most of the food in their full stomachs. Just Rachel, Oli and I remain in the house.

I decided to stay in my study and think of all the great times with the pastor to commemorate his death. After a minute or two, I was fresh out of good memories, so, I decided to drink.

"I think more commemoration is in order. Besides, this is hangover-worthy." I grab my glass and begin to delight my spirits with my choice liquor. "Dead man, it's your day. Happy Death Day, Dad!" I consume half of the gin in the glass and fill it back up. "Dad...dad...how could I ever call you dad? You were just a counterfeit cleric and scummy sperm donor! I hate you! I hate you, and I'm glad you died."

"Oliver, dear, who are you talking to?" Rachel asks from the other side of the door.

"No one," I say with more aggression than ever used before.

"Can I speak with you a moment?"

"Give me a second." I cast my clandestine liquid friend back into its drawer under my desk. "Come in."

"The door is locked; you're going to have to come over to open it."

Oh, hell. This is no good. I'm barely sitting straight up in this chair, let alone walking over to open doors. "Okay." My hands offer their support by digging into the desk to balance me. As I shuffle my feet around the mahogany frame, my hands forget to move, and my body nearly sprawls on the floor—as usual. I regain my stability. Knowing that the door would act as a buttress for my intoxicated state, I lunge towards it.

"Oh, no!" Rachel screams when she hears my body crash against the wooden door. "What happened Oliver? Are you alright?"

"Yes, honey. Everything is just fine," I say, opening the door.

As Rachel walks in, her honeydew aroma is challenged by the stark scent of gin that is occupying my mouth. I try to keep my mouth closed, but she is no novice to my past nightly activities.

"Sit down, Oliver." I stagger to sit in one of the chairs in front of my desk. "I know it's been a tough week. But, baby, you've been shutting yourself in this study every day. We had a house full of people, and you stayed in your study the entire time. Now I smell alcohol on your breath."

"I'm not drunk."

"I didn't say you were drunk. I said I could smell the alcohol on your breath. It's all over you. You can barely walk."

"I'm just fine. Why am I here bothering me? I mean…why you here bothering me?"

"I'm concerned about you. You told me you stopped drinking, but I find you locked in your office smelling like a drunk on one of the corners downtown. You're shutting me out. It's not good to let your emotions fester in you like this, Oliver. You have yet to say a full sentence to me about your father's death."

"He is not my father!"

"Well, whose father is he? He's surely not mine. You sat on the front row with the family at the funeral. You have his first, middle, and last name. So, whose father is he?"

"Rachel, I don't want to talk about this. I refuse."

"You refuse?" She grabs my face under my chin. "Look at me. I'm your wife. We are one. You don't just refuse me from your heart. We've been married almost ten years, and I have never seen you shut me off like this. Talk to me."

"I don't want to talk to me…I mean…you. I want you out of my face."

"I'm not going anywhere. I'm staying in your face. I live in your face. I wash the towels with which you wash your face. I gave birth to our son that has your face. So, honey, I'm staying right here in your face."

She leans forward and puts her hand on mine. I snatch it away and swing at her face with one swift motion. The sound of my open palm against her cheek startles me sober. As her head rocks to the right, I am paralyzed by an array of conflicting emotions. I want to hug her, but, frightened, I jump up and sprint towards the door.

"Where are you going?" Her head snaps back towards my direction. Her logical question interrupts my knee-jerk reaction. "If you leave now, you are leaving forever. I don't want you back if you walk out that door." I turn to see her cupping her bruised cheek turned moist by her tears. I back into the wall and slide down to the floor.

She stands over me, shaking her finger. "Okay. Okay. You've never hit me before, so I'm going to assume you just released some emotion with my face in the way. Maybe I shouldn't have gotten in your face and pressed so hard. Maybe I love you too much."

She freezes like she's stuck in time. She doesn't even blink. I stare at her, not knowing what to say or do. Then, as if she never took a breath, she says, "God knows I love you. But, I know this Oliver Clark, Jr.: I will be the last person you ever hit if you hit me again."

She steps toward the doorway. "I'm sorry," I say like a little child that just spilled the milk.

"I know you are. You can sleep downstairs and sober up." She takes a step forward and pauses. "You better have a damn good sermon tomorrow, because I'm going to need it." Her feet sound like boulders smashing into asphalt as she strides out and slams the door. I hear her bitter footsteps as she slowly walks up the stairs.

My heart is crushed. I just struck the woman I love. Terry was right. I did let my hurt cause those I love pain. What kind of love is that? What kind of husband am I—what kind of pastor? I'm a wife beater. I abused my wife. How could she ever love me again? How can I look at Oli in the face, knowing I slapped his mother?

I slouch there another hour, crying like a lost child. The book. I remember the book and the note that came with it: "It will help you love." I crawl over to the drawer in my desk where I tossed the book and pull it out.

Hours pass. The sun is filtering through the vertical blinds, and, along with the alarm on my phone, it is reminding me that my church service will be starting in a few hours. The unopened book is still lying on the floor beside me. I flip through the pages. I pause at the last chapter, after seeing the title. I breeze through each paragraph but get caught on the author's last words. I keep praying them aloud: "Lord, help me to love above all else. Help me to love above all else."

CHAPTER 5: GLORIA SANCHEZ

When it All Falls Down

∞ ∞ ∞

Today's my anniversary.

Maybe that's why I want to shower even longer. Even though I survived, it's getting harder to do this. I never thought I would still be here. For ten years, the moon has followed me to work, and the sun has guided me home. I've been every man's fantasy, dressing as nurses, officers, and judges. More people have seen my breasts than the ones sold at KFC.

I guess I should be happy. Many of the girls don't make it this long. With drugs and diseases everywhere, I should thank my lucky stars I'm still right in my head. I have a beautiful daughter, a home, and own a truck. I'm okay.

When I walk through my apartment door, I hear Nahlia's T.V. playing. I always thought her sleeping with the T.V. on was just a way to handle being alone at night. I secure the locks and head down the hall to her cracked bedroom door. Peering through, I see one of those early morning televangelists on the screen. He's pacing the floor while holding a coffee table Bible in his hand.

He says, "God can do it. Just trust Him."

Nice suit.

The T.V. hums as I turn it off. Nothing against the minister, but this is how Nahlia trusts that I'm home.

She's fast asleep. With no other sounds around, I listen to Nahlia, my little kitten, purring. I never linger too long. There's a maternal need in me to make sure she's okay. I tiptoe out, shutting her door in the process.

Grabbing the work bag I left at the front door, I enter my bedroom. I open up the bag and take out a brown envelope. It feels like the old wrinkled flesh I had to rub on tonight. Grabbing it, I sit Indian-style on the plum carpet in front of my black safe. No one comes in my home, so hiding the medium-sized safe is pointless. Besides, it would take four wrestlers, two football players, and a boxer to move it. After it opens, I put in the three thousand dollars I just made.

Stain tells us never to trust banks. He likes to say, "No trail, no taxes." Since the first day I started, I haven't put a single dollar bill in the bank. I went and bought this safe, and haven't used anything but cash since then. I carry money and my Smith and Wesson wherever I go, and there has yet to be a problem that either one of them couldn't solve.

I've saved a little over one hundred thousand dollars. Soon, I'm going to move us into the house I've always wanted. We have lived in this crap box for too long. This is all she knows. I want to show her that there is so much more out there. She should be able to go on trips and see the world—Italy, Spain, even New York would be something different.

Sometimes, I sit like this and stare at the money for hours, wondering if it's really worth it. Should I run away with Nahlia to some small city? The problem is that I can't go anywhere without Stain's approval. "You run, and you're done," is all he would say.

I shut the safe.

Standing back up, I now realize just how sore my legs are from a long Friday night of dancing, and prepare to take a hot shower. As the steam starts to build up in the bathroom, I take off my clothes. I don't even change when I leave the club. I just throw on my little black dress and a coat to get home and strip it all away. Looking in the mirror seems to get a bit more comfortable as I stack up more cash. Money tends to make people feel better about themselves, even if they aren't worth the paper it's printed on.

This is almost over.

UNLOVABLE

I feel like my mind refuses to see anything but my twenty-year-old self. The mirror is like a time machine where a younger, more arrogant, and optimistic version of myself stares back at me. In my mind, I owned the world. Well, I guess I actually thought the world owed me. As I pull the coils of my obsidian black hair from my toffee-brown eyes, I gather each strand into a ponytail that brushes against my mid-back.

This is almost over.

The increasing steam invades the bathroom, compromising the view of the younger woman. I wipe the mirror to see if I can get one more glance at my former self, but the image is too distorted. After removing my lingerie, I fit my hair in my shower cap and step into the steamy, refreshingly hot shower. Guys would pay good money to see me dripping with soapy water. But, with all the sensual movements I made tonight, showering is the most tedious yet necessary part of my day.

Like sand on a shore, the water washes over my curvaceous frame, erasing whatever the night left there. If I were on stage, the men would be howling as I swayed my runway model hips, allowing the stream of suds to melt into the rounded slopes of my breasts. My thirty-year-old body still causes even the sexiest twenty-something to stare.

Ending the show, I turn off the water and dry off with a pearl-white economy bath towel. It's the kind of material that gets just as wet as me but still doesn't dry me completely. After slipping into an old t-shirt and shorts, I step out of the bathroom, letting the steam escape in the narrow hallway. The bottom of my feet dry instantly as I walk on the brown shag carpet. Entering the small, dark kitchen, I flick the light switch and grab the kettle to fill with water.

While others need foot massages and backrubs, all I want is some hot peppermint tea after work. Once the water boils, I prepare my cup, bring it into the living room and sink into my favorite chair—an old Powder blue recliner I bought at a yard sale when I first moved in. The tea is too hot to sip but perfect to smell. I place my nose right over the mug and close my eyes. The peppermint's aroma tingles my nose hairs as it fills and refreshes every free space in my head. I take several more whiffs of the tea before placing it on the end table beside me.

Switching on the lamp next to me, I pick up the book beside the tea. Can't say I ever was much of a reader. I can count the books I've read on the one hand, but for some reason, I feel what this author is saying. He might not ever make Oprah's book club or become famous, but his writing sure has kept me sane.

One of the girls who retired from the strip club slipped it to me before she left. The author was a close friend of hers. I guess she could tell from the way I started at the club that I was headed for serious trouble if I didn't stay grounded.

Some people head to church to ease their sorrows and get strength for the next week, but there aren't too many churches ready to welcome my type. So, I made Ernest Lee my preacher, this recliner my pew, and his rare book my song and sermon. It wasn't until the second time I read it that I realized he was actually a minister.

I find that every time I read it, a piece of me gets stronger. It's like he's ministering to me without using any scriptures. I pretend Ernest Lee is sitting next to me with some peppermint tea. He says:

> So, I cry each night, longing for a world that won't hate so much what it doesn't understand. It's as pointless as hating another planet because we don't know what's on it. It's like hating heat because we can't examine the sun's core. I cry, knowing that my brothers and sisters—of all colors, creeds, and compositions—and I lose control of fragments of our humanity when we are infected by the viral surge of hate. Often, we are infected unaware, driven by its procreator—fear—and offspring—judgment and unforgiveness.

I don't know if it's the warmth of the peppermint tea, the comfort of the recliner or the soothing of my soul that Ernest provides, but soon I'm fast asleep.

The sound of Nahlia's alarm is like a shot of caffeine to my system. I'm hopping out of my chair, sore legs and all, and dashing to the kitchen to cook us a great Saturday morning breakfast. She doesn't like using the alarm on Saturdays, but she knows I want us to start our days together. She's the only family I have—her and Ernest Lee.

UNLOVABLE

§§§§§

I hate hospitals. Stain has me here to get tested for STDs. He watched some report on 20/20, and now he has all the girls getting tested today. He says, "I can't have girls that can drop dead on me. If you want to drop dead, you can do it on your own time. I need girls that plan on living. So, all of you are getting tested if you're going to work here."

They had me put something in my mouth and put it in a solution. I'm supposed to get my results in about twenty minutes. For now, I wait. Stain must not like hospitals, because he had all the girls come in at the same time. It was kind of like a reunion. We just looked at each other. Some smiled; others glared. I just kept my head down. I was already the last one to arrive. Stain snarled at me when I walked in.

Out of the twelve girls, one, Déjà Wu, had already run out crying. Stain didn't even follow her out to make sure she was okay. The three girls left and I look at each other and shake our heads, knowing we will never see her again. All I know about her is that she's Chinese, and I hate her name.

The commotion makes all of us a bit uneasy. When the next girl is called to the back, she looks scared. One of the girls left in the waiting room starts sweating like she is running miles on a hot summer's day. The other is getting fidgety, tapping her foot and playing with her hair while humming. After a while, Stain snarls at her, "Girl, if you don't stop, I'm going to rip out that damn weave." She gets so still I want to walk over and make sure she's still alive.

Soon the rest of the girls walk into the back and come out with smiles on their faces. I'm a little jittery now myself. I doubt I have anything in my blood that's not supposed to be there, but Stain isn't making the pressure any easier. Before Stain can say anything to me, the nurse is calling my name. Since I'm the last one, Stain gets up to go with me.

"Right this way," says the nurse pointing down the hall. She leads us into an examining room. "Here we are. The doctor will be in momentarily." The nurse closes the door as she walks out.

"I'm so glad this is about to be over," Stain says, leaning back with a sigh. "This took almost all day. I have to get back to the club to do some work."

"Well, you asked for this Stain," I say, trying not to sound sarcastic. "These things take time." He grumbles and closes his eyes.

We sit in silence until the door opens. "Good day, everyone. I'm Dr. Talbot." As he walks in and sits on the circular stool, I notice he isn't making any eye contact. "Ms. Sanchez, you have the option of hearing these results alone."

"Doc," Stain says before I can respond, "anything you have to say to her you can say to me." The doctor looks at me. I nod my head.

"Well, your sample came back. You tested positive for HIV."

Stain jumps up. "What the hell? Are you kidding me?"

"Sir, calm down."

"There is no calm in this. Cunt, who you been screwing? HUH?" I can't say anything. I can barely breathe. With my hands covering my face, I can still tell that he is standing over me ready to spew fire. "How long has she had this?"

"Well, Gloria, when was your last HIV test?" the doctor asks me.

"Ten years," I say through my tear-soaked palms.

"Well, when was your last sexual encounter?"

"Goddamn bitch," Stain says as he storms out of the office.

"Well, I'm glad he is gone," the doctor says, moving closer to me. So, when did you last have sex?"

"About two months ago…with him."

"Oh, I see. Was it protected or unprotected?"

"Unprotected, but he's been the only man I've been with since I gave birth to my daughter. I've never had another man since then. How could this have happened to me?"

"How old is your daughter?"

"She is nine, almost ten."

"So, if I understand correctly, you haven't had sex with anyone else besides him in almost ten years?" I nod my head up and down. "Okay. I need to make sure he hasn't left the building. I'll be right back." I cry even harder after he leaves.

What is this? Is this some punishment? Is this what I deserve for dancing in front of men—a death sentence? What about Nahlia? How will I take care of her now? I thought I mastered crying about something when I left home each night to work. There was no way of knowing I was a novice at tears until now. Alone in this room, I am crying like a newborn with no awareness of self-control or self-esteem.

§§§§§

Three hours later, I'm leaving the hospital. They drew some blood, and I waited for a specialist to come over and talk with me. She gave me some comfort, but I'm still sobbing. I'm thirty and just found out I'm HIV positive. There's no way I can get Nahlia a daddy now. I hear her praying for one before she goes to bed at night. She has known Stain all her life, but he never really spends time with us.

I pull up to the apartment complex and notice Nahlia sitting outside. When she sees my truck, she runs towards me. "Mom, Mom!"

"What's wrong, Nahlia?"

"Stain just left. He came in and said we couldn't stay here anymore. He came with six other big guys and moved out everything. How can he do that?"

I know Nahlia's not lying, but I don't believe her. I sprint upstairs and find my door still open. Besides the paper and clothes lying around the room, the area is bare. I head to my room. The safe is open. I fall on my knees and look in. It was just as empty as the day I bought it. How could anyone have gotten in it? I'm the only one that knew the combination.

"Mom, come and see this!"

I want to break down, but I have my daughter to worry about now. Getting up, I check on Nahlia. She's holding a piece of paper. "What's that, kitten?"

"It's a note. You want me to read it?"

"Go ahead."

"It says, 'Gloria. We're through. This is my apartment, so get the hell out today.'"

"Nahlia," I say, reaching for the note, "Let me read that." I take the letter and begin reading to myself:

> Gloria. We're through! This is my apartment, so get the hell out today. I'm taking back everything I ever gave you, including that money I let you earn. I better not ever see you again. You're getting off easy.

I let all the air out of my helpless body. I stand there—lost. How is this my life? I want to believe it's all a dream. I want to scream. This can't be happening to me right now. Hopelessness rises in me like yeast.

I feel faint.

Nahlia takes the note from my hand and hugs me. Nahlia and I hug often, but this is something different. Her hug seems motherly and safe. After a moment, I say, "Nahlia, I need to go take care of this."

"Mom...no! I don't want you getting hurt or in more trouble with him. We'll be okay."

I wish I believed that. "Kitten, your mom needs to make things okay. If there are still trash bags under the sink, grab them, and put all your clothes in them."

An hour later, everything we owned is in my truck, and we are pulling up to Platinum Dolls. The club doesn't open for another three hours, so most of the staff isn't here. I park my truck in the front. "Kitten, if anything happens; don't let anyone put a hand on you. Okay?"

"Mom, I don't like this. What are you about to do?"

"Just let mommy handle this. I love you," I say, kissing her on the forehead.

"I love you too, Mom."

The bouncer stops me once I walk through the door. "You can't come in, Gloria."

"Oh, what you can't call me Elle anymore?"

"Stain gave you that name. He's taking it back."

After I started reading Ernest Lee's book, I pledged not to curse, smoke, or drink, but today doesn't count. "Fuck you, Rashad! Get the hell out of my way." My knee to his groin stops his attempt to grab me. I run down the back hallway to Stain's office. I pull out my gun. When I open the door, I see him sitting at his desk, counting money.

"I can't believe you actually came here," he says, looking up at me. "Didn't I tell you that I better not see you again? Is that a...a gun in your hand?" He sounds like the devil when he laughs.

"I want my money."

"What? This money?" he asks, waving his hands over the money on the desk.

"How did you get it? I'm the only one who knew the combination," I say.

"You should know by now that I like to know everything about my girls. You lived in my apartment, remember? All you need to know is that I was watching."

I lunge forward to grab some money, but his hand snags my arm, making the gun fall to the floor. He stands up and walks around his desk. "You should have run."

I do something I have dreamed of doing since I met him—spit right in his mouth.

He brings his hand across my face. He only slapped me clean across my face once, but this is different. He balls his fist and hits me like a man. He roars as his limb swings through the air. The blow sends me flying back. His grip on my wrist keeps me from slamming into the ground. I just hang there like a pool noodle. "You wanna come to my club and steal from me? You wanna put your infected spit in my mouth? I'm gonna kill you girl."

As he lets go of my wrist, I try to get back to my feet. I didn't feel the pain of his blow right away, but, when I was halfway to my feet, it struck me like lightning across my jaw. It hurt so bad I lost my balance again and fell back on my head.

"You sorry bitch. I can't believe I wasted ten years on you." He takes his pointed alligator boot and slams it into my side. I scream out in pain, as I feel like some organ just burst open.

I hear the door open and soon know that Rashad has just walked in.

They beat me like eggs.

During a part of it, I prayed to be knocked unconscious, but God must still be mad with me. I felt every blow. Stain only stopped hitting me because he hates to get sweaty. "Get her out of here."

"Where do you want me to put her?"

"You know where to put trash."

Rashad tosses me over his massive shoulder. The blood from my face disappears in his black shirt. He carries me all the way back down the hall. "You should have listened Gloria. I didn't wanna do that."

I just moan. The pain of his shoulder blade digging into my stomach is unbearable.

When we reach the front door, he tosses me to the ground. Nahlia sees my battered body and jumps out of the truck. "Mom! Mom! What happened?"

"Get me outta here," I say, moaning. Nahlia tries to help me to my feet but ends up dragging me to the truck door. Everything hurts, but I know I can't stay here. I shriek as the pain shoots through my tender body. Even the car seat feels like a bed of broken glass and nails.

Nahlia doesn't even ask; she just starts the truck. Her foot can barely reach the pedal. "Where?" I hear the fear in her angelic voice.

"Just go!"

§§§§§

Chapter 6: Oliver Clark, Jr.

September Valentine

I close the book.

After sitting there staring at the last page, shutting it seems almost as much of an achievement as reading it for the fifth time this week. I stare at the front cover like the gloss is hypnotizing me. Its surface is void of any activity or semblance of expression—no words, no pictures. There is just blank space.

I have asked myself countless times: Who writes a book with nothing on the cover? Several times I contemplated drawing something to occupy the space, but the urge seems to dissipate by the time I grab a marker. What kind of depiction would I etch on another person's book anyway?

By the fifth reading, I believe I finally discern the reality behind its emptiness. The truth is the cover is a cover; it's a farce—much like my life. Inside are pages filled with pain, shame, and remorse; however, the whiteness of the cover purports the illusion that all is well. The cover on the book is as much a mirage as the surface of my life. I walk around like a holy figure dressed in white. The reality is I have my issues that mire my purity.

"Pastor Clark," Rachel says, startling me as she stands in front of my desk. I inhale through my nose, gasping so hard that I feel near faint. The expression of apathy is molded like clay on a sculpture, which leads me to believe that her stealth was intentional.

It's been a week since I struck her face. She hasn't spoken to me; I haven't looked at her. Now, she is perched in front of my desk. "I'm sorry." Not only is she reusing my words, but she is also mimicking the same tone and facial gestures I used after I slapped her.

"It's quite alright, Rachel," I say, knowing nothing is right at this moment.

"May I sit?"

A small puff of air escapes through my taut lips, as I chuckle to myself.

The games have indeed begun.

My hand motions like a crossing guard directing traffic. She nods, positioning herself in the chair across from my desk. The third hand on the wall clock makes its full rotation. We sit as distant lovers separated by a chasm of emotions. The desk stands in proxy for the rift between our souls. Staring into each other's eyes, we are struck by the silence. With a mechanical grace, she leans back and crosses her girlishly thick legs, letting her sundress drift down from her knee. Even around the house, she dresses like she is going to a church picnic.

"So, Mr. Clark," Rachel says, sounding like a detective ready to crack a case.

"Yes, Mrs. Clark."

"Your sermon went well Sunday."

"Thank you for being there."

"Well, why wouldn't I be there? You know it is just as much my church as it is yours." Her response is more emotional than I'm sure she desired.

She pauses. Her shapely chest and shoulders slouch and regain composure with one deep breath. "I found the themes of love and forgiveness to be very...appropriate. Were you working on that sermon long?"

She is attempting to bait me to reveal if the sermon was specifically for her or just the message that was next in line. I shake my head and laugh. "Mrs. Clark—honey—you are so cute." Her face is unaffected. "I mentioned during the message that I was drawing a great deal from a book I read."

She nods in agreement. "I recall that. We should have this author over for dinner if he inspires you to preach like that."

I nod back, saying, "I would second that sentiment if he weren't deceased."

"Oh, okay. Well, what made you read the book?"

"In all actuality, my love for you was the motivation to read the book."

Her eyebrow twitches. I can tell she is holding back her emotions like a dam. She wants control—craves it.

"You are the motivation for everything I love and hold dear. I only wish I could show you how much your love means to me. No gem, no diamond, no pearl could ever denote the depth of my love for you."

It is like watching a mannequin come to life. Her ruby red lips begin to pucker, and her nose flares. The minute her tender eyes soften, her dam collapses. A single tear rolls down her round, roughed cheek. She wipes it away before it passes her taut mouth.

"Rachel Clark, I have loved you since the moment I saw your soft, caramel-colored eyes. Right now, even the effervescent aroma of your skin makes my heart want to be near you and hands long to caress your body. It hurts that I hurt you. What I did to you was wrong."

"You're damn right it was. You hit me. Have I led you to believe that flattery and a simple apology would solve all of this after a whole week of you not saying anything to me?" I try to speak, but she abruptly interrupts me. "Are you so arrogant to think I won't leave you? You don't speak to me for a week? I have to walk into your study and confront you? I may love you, but I love me enough to know when I've had enough."

"Rachel, what are you saying?"

"I'm saying that your eloquent words mean nothing to me."

"Look," I say to her, as I move to the chair beside her. "I couldn't even look at you all week. It wasn't arrogance; it was shame. You have a right to leave me, but you would only create a huge void in my world if you did. Tell me what to say. Tell me what to do. I'll do it."

"Give up the alcohol."

"Done. I already stopped drinking."

"I mean it." As she rocks her head from side to side, her manicured hands are flinging tears from her face. "You have to promise me."

"I promise," I say with a soap opera star's passion.

"No! You have to promise me for real. No more drinking. I can't take it anymore. This family can't take it, Oliver. You have got to promise me." She nearly chokes on the steady stream of tears rushing down her flushed face. The emotion in the room swells like an ocean's wave. Soon my knees are like anchors falling against the wooden floors. I sail to her, landing my head on the shores of her warm lap. "Promise me!"

I lift my head and peer into her eyes. "I promise. I'm so sorry."

I continue to offer apologies and beg forgiveness until my throat is bone dry. Rachel takes her thumbs and wipes away my tears, somehow not slicing me with her lengthy pale pink nails. As I close my eyes, I feel her gentle fingers as she holds my head. I always feel safe with Rachel. It pains my heart to know that I violated the security she felt with me.

Her warm lips press against my forehead. As she pulls back, she says, "I pray you mean it." She leans in and kisses the same spot. This time she lingers. The aromatic smell of vanilla invades my nostrils. All I can do is breathe in her love.

I inhale until there is no more space in me to consume her. I feel like a glutton. Not wanting to exhale, I horde her scent. Just before I lose all sensibility, she pushes me away and stands to her feet. Looking at me sprawled on the floor, she says, "I pray you mean it."

Her house shoes sound like combat boots against the wood floors. I can't help but consider that she just won this game. With the grin engraved on my face, this is the first time that I am elated to lose.

As she turns her head, she flips her long, shiny twists and snaps her eyes at me over her shoulder. "I want to say: I love you, and I'm here for you. I'm always here for you." She flashes a smile and exits the room.

I remain on the floor, looking at the door that has now closed behind her. I love her more now than ever. I finally appreciate how much it means to have someone like that on the other side of my study door.

The door comes ajar again, and Rachel's head pokes through. "Oh, and just in case you weren't sure, I definitely could use some flowers and chocolate." I join her as she snickers like a schoolgirl and shuts the door.

UNLOVABLE

I guess I need to be finding my shoes.

§§§§§

With Oli gone on a camping trip in the mountains, I officially record today as the quietest Saturday since he was born nine years ago. Except for the sobs and laughter that Rachel and I exchanged earlier, there was relative silence in our home. There are no sounds of early morning cartoons, no explosions or screams on video games. No doorbells are ringing by neighborhood children inquiring if Oli can go outside and play.

Only the sounds of Rachel and I are heard in the house. The most noise I made was in the garage when I went to and came from the store in my SUV. She was noiseless until two hours ago. After that, I hear the sounds of pots and pans clanging, grease sizzling and Rachel humming like her mother, Gwen, while cooking.

"Oliver, you can come out and eat now."

"I'm on my way."

Curiosity grips me like a sumo wrestler. She tells me to stay in my study while she cooks. Shocked wouldn't really be the word to use, maybe nervous. She only cooks for Sunday dinner. She forgave me much quicker than I expected, which has my imagination starting to get the best of me. Is she trying to poison me with food while Oli is away? Is she going to strangle me from behind while I eat one of my favorite dishes? My mind wanders deeper into more irrational thoughts taken from some of my favorite horror movies.

I shake my head and laugh at myself. Not Rachel. While she is fierce and opinionated, she has a docile humility and overall affability. I saunter out of the office and down the hallway through the dark kitchen. The smell of used grease is prevalent in the air.

"Rachel? Where are you?" I fumble for the lights. My hand only feels a covering where the light switch should be located.

"I'm back here, Oliver. Don't try to turn on the lights; there's tape over them. Just follow my voice."

My steps slow to a crawl.

"Come on, Oliver. You're almost there."

I know the layout of my kitchen, but my thoughts are returning back to their fear-mongering. There might be a mousetrap, bear trap or some other trap waiting on me. I drag my feet across the linoleum floor, hoping to feel something before it causes me harm. With great relief, I make it to the other side. I notice the flicker of light on the wall ahead. "I'm over here, dear."

As I turn the corner, I see portions of my wife exposed by the tall, slim candle situated in the middle of the dining room table. Three more lit candles lay across the mantle that sits just behind her. "Rachel...what is all of this?"

"Come, sit down and eat." I can see well enough in the dimly lit room to know there is nothing hazardous on the floor. I dash to the chair, lifting it and slamming it on the ground before sitting. I can see Rachel's puzzled face in the candlelight. "What was that about?"

"Oh, just checking." Yeah, I was checking alright. I needed to make sure there was no weak leg on the chair.

"Checking for what, Oliver?"

"Termites."

"Okay—well, I have prepared a beautiful meal for you tonight, if I must say so myself." I stretch my neck like a turtle lifting its head out of its shell. She begins opening each container and pausing to let me savor the thought of consumption. "I made some mouth-watering barbeque baked chicken and candied yams. These steamed string beans are fresh from my garden in the backyard. Here's some super cheesy macaroni and cheese and seasoned steamed cabbage. I know you love Texas toast, so I made sure to prepare that. Last but not least, I made your favorite dessert." I gulp. She uncovers the last container. "I made this strawberry cheesecake from scratch. I hope you enjoy."

I am dazed. Rachel has arrayed the table with her grandmother's china. With all of my favorite foods staring at me, my brain is still resistant. "Are you going to eat?"

"Of course, I am." As she stands, I notice she is wearing a black dress as tight as Fort Knox security. She lifts my plate and begins to scoop ample portions of each item on it. Setting it down, she looks at me and says, "I'm so glad we are alone today, Mr. Clark." Beads of sweat begin to form on my upper lip. I'm clutching the sides of the plate. I'm hungry but attempting to withstand feelings of trepidation that are taking root in my stomach. She steps behind me and positions her mouth next to my ear. "Come on, and eat up."

Rachel grabs my jittery hand, helping me to pick up my fork. "If you are shaking now, you're really going to be shaking after you taste this." She directs my hand to gather some candied yams. My mouth is still shut tight. Thinking it is open, she thrusts the fork forward. I scream in pain as she jabs the underside of my lip. Bloodied yams are now rolling down my white t-shirt, landing in my lap. "Oliver, are you okay?"

She reaches for my dinner napkin and proceeds to wipe off the yams. Since I am still holding my lip, I quietly groan, grabbing the napkin from her. I cover the stab wound with it.

"Why did you have your mouth closed?" She finally realizes that she isn't entirely at fault in this debacle. "Huh?" She takes a few steps around to look me in my eyes.

"You can still talk. I didn't take off your lip. It was only a fork, not a butcher's knife." I stare at her as if she was a ghost. I can tell she is becoming more annoyed as I prolong my answer. She begins to swing her arms, hopelessly. "Okay, Oliver. I'm done. I tried. Have a good night."

"Wait—," I say knowing she won't receive the truth any better than my silence. "I...I was afraid."

"Afraid? What were you afraid of, Oliver?" She shakes her head so hard I think it might pop off.

"I was afraid you might be trying to hurt me," I say looking away.

Rachel prances behind me, laughing. "Are you serious? I can't believe you actually thought that." Rachel returns her mouth to my ear. Her now sinister laughter is so extreme my eardrum feels like it might rupture. "I would never do that to you, Oliver," she says, placing her arm over my shoulder. "I love you." I detect a slight hint of sarcasm in her voice. "But, if I were going to hurt you, I might do this," she says as her arm locks around my neck like a noose.

I attempt to grab her body, but she dodges my hands as they come near her. "Is this about right, honey?" I only squirm more. "Yeah, this is how it's done on those Lifetime movies. "But—" she says as she releases her hold. "I'm not a Lifetime kind of lady. Now, where are my flowers, my funny little Valentine?"

I'm still holding my chest, catching my breath, so I point towards the front of the house.

"They are…ugh…in the…office."

"Wonderful. I have such a wonderful husband, considering."

"Considering?" I dig my heels into the floor and push back from the table to stand up. "Considering what?" She takes the bloody napkin from my hand and examines my chin.

"You bleed so easily."

She pats the underside of my lip a few times. "Well, at least your body heals itself pretty quick. I can deal with that." As I stand up, she notices the stains from where the candied yams plopped on my clothes. "Oh, this won't do. Not for my September Valentine's Day. We're going to have to get you out of these clothes, Mr. Clark."

"Honey, I'm not worried about my clothes. I want to make sure this food doesn't get cold."

"We can always reheat it." She begins to tug at my shirt, lifting it up to my chest. When she notices that my arms are still dangling at my sides, she tosses me a look that makes my arms rise like she just pulled a gun on me. "That's better." She flings the shirt to the floor and slaps my smooth, bare chest with her hands. "Did you really want to marry me?"

My face squints at the randomness of this question. "Now, why would you ask me a question like that?"

"Just answer the question, Clark." Just as she prepares to deliver another playful strike to my chest, I clutch her hips and pull her towards me.

"Of course, I wanted to marry you. Now, why would you ask me that?"

"Well, I always thought your father made you marry me when he found out I was pregnant with Oli. He probably wouldn't have let you be pastor otherwise, right?"

I grab her tighter. "Look at me in my eyes, Rachel."

She shifts her stare from my chest to the place where it feels like she stabbed me. "Honey…my eyes." Her hesitance proves just how nervous she is about my response. "You are absolutely right. My father did tell me that the only way I could inherit the church was to marry you. I must say it was the one thing my father instructed of me that I was happy to do." Her eyes begin to sparkle. "Do you remember the day I proposed?"

"Yeah, you were sweating like you had just preached a revival."

"I was sweating because I was nervous about proposing to the woman of my dreams. My father only pushed me to do what I wanted to do anyway. I can honestly say it was the second happiest day of my life."

"Aww baby, that's sweet," she says, sliding her arms up to my chest until they lock together around my neck. "Hold up. What is first?"

"The day you said, 'I do.'"

She stares into my eyes a moment. I think she may have expected me to chuckle or do something else to indicate I am joking. After she scans my eyes for sincerity, she tugs the back of my neck down and places her tender lips against mine. The present fades into eternity as her silky lips seem to absolve the gravity of previous offenses. The deeper I press into them, the more it feels like aloe vera is being applied to my sin-burnt soul.

She is healing me. So many questions begin to flood my mind that my mouth busts open. I snatch my head away from her. "Why do you still love me?"

She only grins and pulls me back to her lips. Pulling back again, I ask," Seriously, why do you still love me?"

"Oliver," she says, as she steps forward, knocking me back down into the chair. "You told me that no matter what you would be there, and you have never broken your promise."

She spreads her legs and hops on my lap. "When I came to the church, you were there to help me get off drugs. You were there sneaking me into your parent's house when my mother wouldn't let me in the house at night. You were there at the altar showing me love when your father was calling me 'black street trash.' You stood up for me. So, not loving you doesn't seem fair, now does it?"

"Well, when you put it that way—"

"Shh," she says, placing her finger over my mouth. "Enough talk. Did you get my September Valentine's Day candy?" I moan as her hands trail over my nipples. "Well, did you get them?" Her hands travel until they grasp my belt buckle. "Did you?"

"Yeah. I got them. They are with the—"

"Shh," she says, tracing my lips with her finger while loosening my belt. "Let me have some fun finding them. In fact, why don't you hide too? We can play a little Hide n' Seek. Oh, this is going to be too much fun." She pushes back and stands up. "Okay, go hide while I cover the food."

"I'm hungry. Why would I want to play this game?"

"Well, baby, how do you like this dress?" Breaking into a smile, her enticing, dazzling white teeth light up the room. Her full-figured frame preserves the curves positioned in places that make men's temperatures rise.

"I love it. You look phenomenal. I could stare at you all night."

"Well, I don't want to be your mannequin; I want to be your lover. Besides, this dress looks even better on the floor." She winks. Her pencil-thin eyebrows arch down to her long, shadowy eyelashes. I hop out of the chair and dart towards the kitchen. "Hold up, mister." I stop and look back at her. "Drop those pants."

§§§§§

The rising sun causes flickers of light to loiter around my inactive eyelids. The room's silence agrees with my weary body. "Just lay here," they say, wooing me back to the threshold of my dreams.

UNLOVABLE

If it weren't for the persistent pestering of brilliant rays flashing across my eyes, I would have stayed in my slumber. As my eyes twitch, the brittle crust in the corners proves to be an irritation. I begin to rub my eyes, which only further awakens my body. Confident that all of the morning crust is removed, I stretch my arms and sit up.

Being that it is Sunday, I expect to awaken in my king-sized bed upstairs. As I peruse my surroundings, nothing around me reminds me of my bedroom. The three candles on the mantle have melted down to near non-existence. The candle on the dining room table is missing. As I attempt to retrace the events of last night, I remember Rachel commanding me to drop my pants. I ran and hid in the closet because I couldn't fit under the bed. She crept past the hall closet I was hiding in and found the candy and flowers.

I heard her shout, "I found the presents, so I win. If I find you, I get to have you however I want." The sound of doors slamming was getting closer to my closet, and I knew she would soon find me. When she reached my door, she knocked and said, "I'll be in the dining room when you're ready."

After ten minutes of hearing no movement around the door, I decided to step out. I walked back through the kitchen and saw the same flickering light, but this time it was much brighter. When Rachel saw me stroll into the dining room, she said, "Come here, baby." She was stretched across our air mattress on her stomach, seductively eating the chocolates I bought. "I sure could use your help getting out of this dress." Moving closer, I realized that the petals of the flowers I purchased were spread across the mattress.

Throughout the next several hours, I heard high notes that sounded eerily like Mariah Carey. The candle was knocked over and set fire to the comforter, which is why there is now a gaping hole in it. I got two cramps and nearly choked when Rachel tried to feed me chocolate in the dark.

I look over at the wall clock. 6:50 am. I lie back and turn towards Rachel, who is sleeping on her side. I scoot closer until her heel is resting on the top of my foot. Pulling back her shimmery twists, my lips greet her warm neck, as my right hand slides down her soft side. Her neck becomes moist with my kisses. She eases awake with a moan. "Good morning, Ms. Bunny."

She softly clears her throat. "Good morning, Mr. Egg. Nice night, huh?"

"Yeah. You made me hatch enough times. I don't think I have any more yoke left."

"Alright, that just sounds nasty in the morning," she says, laughing as she rolls onto my stomach.

"Rachel, I just want to thank you for last night."

"And to what do I owe the honor of such thanks?" I squirm as her glossy index fingers proceed to circle my nipples.

"You put in a special effort last night to make it memorable. You really didn't have to do that."

"Oh, Oliver, I did. I want our marriage to last for as long as we do. Besides, I like wearing my big church hats and flashy dresses. I could do without one thing that I know you can help me with."

I look at her and say, "Anything. What can I do? I love you."

"I love you more." She reaches down and gives me a sloppy kiss that has us both chuckling as we wipe our mouths. "Well, you could stop thinking I'm trying to kill you," she says, pinching my nipples like she has two big clamps.

I scream out in pain. "Okay. Okay. Okay. I'll stop." I spin on top of her, positioning myself between her bare legs. I stare into the eyes of the only woman I have loved since I was in college. My body begins to respond to our mutual nakedness.

"Mr. Egg," she says, taunting me. "It appears you have some more in you. What do you say? How about one more go at it?"

"Ms. Bunny, no tricks this time, because you might just make me cancel church today."

§§§§§

CHAPTER 7: GLORIA SANCHEZ

Sabbath Surprises

∞ ∞ ∞

I escaped from the Emergency room.

I didn't tell Nahlia that. I told her that after my examination, finding no significant injuries, they said I was free to go. The first part of that was real, at least. I grabbed Nahlia and put my hand around her mouth when she started shouting, "It's a miracle! It's a miracle!" I couldn't help but agree. I didn't have one broken bone or damaged organ. They told me I was just extremely bruised and sore. I knew I would be even sorer when the police came and asked what happened to me, so I had Nahlia find a wheelchair and roll me out to the truck.

"Mom, where are we going?" I look at her and open my mouth to speak, but nothing comes out. I'm lost. We have no food, money, or shelter. Turning from her, I start up the truck. I can tell she is staring at me, just waiting for me to come up with a great idea. "Mom?"

"I don't know." Hearing those words from my lips sends my aching body into a fit of depression. I finally realize how bad off we are. My body rests on the steering wheel like it's a life preserver. Nahlia slides across the cloth seats, throwing her arm around my waist and head on my shoulder. "I don't know what to do," I say, as the pain in my body is absorbed by the agony in my heart. "We have nowhere to go."

Nahlia hugs me tighter.

Soon my head is resting on Nahlia's thigh, as her fingers are combing through my hair like she's petting a furry dog. I'm not sure when I fell asleep; I just know I'm shaking from a dream about killer clowns.

"Mom, are you okay?"

"Yeah," I say while taking a deep breath. "How long was I asleep?" I'm really wondering why it seems like everything in my world feels like it's falling apart. Even my dreams aren't safe.

"You were out for about three hours. It's a little after 9 am now." I didn't plan on sleeping in the parking garage of a hospital. Hell, I didn't plan on any of this. I'd take fighting killer clowns over this life any day. "Mom, can I ask you a question?"

"Sure, kitten. What is it?"

"Can we go to church today?"

She's never been to a church. I've only gone once myself. Most times, the church would come to me. All kinds of religious people would either come to my club or try to pick me up on the street. The women looked at me crazy and talked about me when I came to church, but after service, their husbands were trying to get with me. I couldn't deal with all the hypocrisy.

"Why do you want to go?"

"I thought we might need it right about now," she says. "Besides, I've kinda wanted to go for a little while, but I knew you wouldn't. I thought maybe today would be different."

Sometimes I wonder who the parent really is.

A part of me hates the idea of even walking into a church. It feels like I'd be agreeing with the lies those holy people try to keep going. Another part of me is just searching for any way to make Nahlia happy right now. "Kitten, look at me. I'm in no shape to go to that fashion show they call church."

She stops rubbing my head and says, "Mom, the preacher said, 'It doesn't matter how you come to church as long as you come.' You have clothes in the back to change into to." Everything in me seems to be in opposition to the thought of walking through church doors.

My throat is as dry as the Sahara desert.

After I let out my third deep sigh, Nahlia says, "Just forget it."

"No, Nahlia, I want to go. I just—"

"Great!" Her excitement makes me sit straight up, with my head shooting out of her lap. "Mom, you're still so jumpy."

Of course, I'm jumpy. Nahlia is acting like she just forgot I was beaten by the man I once thought I loved. I want to curse, but I bite my tongue. I can't be smart with her right now.

"So, what church are we going to, kitten?"

"It's Greater Mount Pleasant Baptist Church."

"Is that the big one on T.V.?"

She looks at me and smiles, saying, "Yep. I was hoping you would know it. I would leave on the T.V. every night so you could see it."

I can't cry now.

No matter how much I fail her, no matter what I do, she still loves me. Ernest Lee was right: "No matter what we lose, we can still find joy in what we have left." As gratitude begins to hug my bitter heart, a strange joy creeps over me like fog. I didn't expect to smile for a while, but Nahlia has done the unexpected once again.

"Well, I guess I will finally get to see this church in person."

"I think we're going to like it," she says.

"If you like it, I'm sure I'll love it." As I turn away from her to look out my side window, my eye catches a glimpse of myself in the rearview mirror. I can't say that last night was my first beating, but it was definitely the worst. My swollen face is one bloody puffy taco. I pat it with my hands. "I just don't know how much they will love me."

I had one miracle happen in the last twenty-four hours. With all the makeup in the back, maybe I can squeeze out one more wonder.

§§§§§

We pull up to this stadium called a church. I swear there are more parking spaces here than the basketball arena downtown. It is so big they have police officers and parking attendants directing traffic. There are even letters on the scattered light poles so you can remember where you parked. I look at Nahlia, "Are you sure we are going to a church?"

"Mom, stop being silly." The attendant directs us down row five of section 'L.' As we drive around, I notice all kinds of cars: Range Rovers, Maseratis, Hondas, and hoopties. Most of the expensive cars are parked in reserved spaces. "Mom, you've driven most of these cars."

There is so much I could say that nothing comes out. I just join her in laughter. We park in the last spot at the end of the row.

As I slam the rusty door shut, Nahlia says, "See, mom, we are dressed just fine for church." She is right. The woman pushing the stroller is about Nahlia's height and looks like she might be just a few years older. Her miniskirt has so much thigh showing that I could have worn it on stage any night. I moan to myself as I take Nahlia's hand and grip it tightly.

Walking past nearly a hundred cars, I can't help but think that I just changed in a Burger King restroom for this. If I really could have it my way, I would be in a warm jacuzzi with Epsom salt. Instead, I had to wash my face in the sink of a fast food joint with a 'C' rating from the Health Department. Lo and behold, I bump into an old client. This is why I don't go out on Sunday mornings. I guess he was getting his old man biscuit and coffee before church. Just before he could see me walk out the front door, I pulled my sunhat down over my face and slid on my broadest and darkest sunglasses.

As we reach the reserved spaces, I notice the same Escalade parked there like the one at Burger King. I freeze. "I can't do this."

"Mom, what's wrong now?"

"I just can't do this," I say, shouting as I walk back down the aisle to my rusty, red Chevy.

"Well, where else are we going to go then?" The people passing by were as nosey as expected. Some actually slowed down to try to look at my face.

UNLOVABLE

"What are you looking at, sunshine?" I say to the woman dressed in yellow that has slowed down so much I think she is about to take my temperature.

"Stop, mom! You're embarrassing me," Nahlia says, running over to me and pulling me between two cars. The woman speeds up while looking back. I'm pretty sure she was making sure I wasn't coming after her.

"I'm afraid I might know some people here." That isn't usually a problem when you are referring to the church, but in my case it is. Nahlia is only nine, but she is sharper than most kids her age.

"If they know you then I guess they will be just as embarrassed, so come on."

She doesn't even wait for my response before she turns and heads towards the large glass doors of the church. I take a minute and make sure my wig is on straight, and my hat and glasses are covering the rest of my face. Realizing that Nahlia has yet to look back, I do my best to walk briskly in my Manolo pumps. What can I say; it is a fashion show after all.

Walking through the doors of the church is odd. These three people are standing there giving out hugs as they welcome everyone inside. I just nod and maneuver around the closest hugging woman. I haven't seen cleavage that deep since Kandy Kane got those implants and forgot to buy new clothes before coming to the club. This woman's breasts are unmistakably real. They don't quite have the lift they probably used to when she wasn't in her late forties.

Nahlia is standing just behind the greeters. I can tell she is frustrated I wouldn't hug the woman back. "I'm still sore," is all I say and keep walking. After we make our way past the first line of defense, two ladies are poking out their chests to show their black badges with white letters with one word inscribed: Usher.

I can't say I know what an usher is. I know the singer, but I doubt he would be giving us a program of the service and leading us to two open seats. Unfortunately, the seats I have in mind are upstairs in the balcony, but it is too late. Nahlia is practically on the usher's heel to sit as close as possible. As we pass the middle mark of the church, which is a feat by itself, I start to get more nervous.

"Ma'am. Ma'am. Excuse me. I'm sure you know how to do your job, but this just isn't going to work."

The usher turns and looks at me cross-eyed as if I just insulted her whole world. "What's wrong with up here?"

"Well, it's too close," I say without flinching—not that anyone could see it through my hat and glasses. "This is the fourth row."

"Dear, you are late. Service is halfway over. These are two of the last seats in the building."

I probably should have just sat down, but the choir was up singing "How Great Thou Art," and it wasn't like people could hear us with all the noise of the singers and instruments.

"I'm about to sweat already from these stadium concert lights you have, and you're telling me in this big 'ole place you can't find two chairs in the back."

"Yes, there are two chairs in the back, if you don't mind sitting on someone's lap," she says with a smirk that I want to remove with the back of my hand.

"Look here you little—"

"Mom," Nahlia says, tugging on my wrist to gain my attention, "I want to sit here. Please?" I can't even blink hard before the usher is storming past the halfway mark again. I turn back to look at Nahlia and find I am the only one standing here.

Nahlia has already said "Excuse me" over a dozen times to get to the seats. It feels like coming into a movie that has already started and trying to take positions in the middle. I bump into several knees before resting my sore hips next to her. She leans over to me, whispering, "Don't ruin this moment for me," and sits back up as if her word is final.

I don't have much tongue left to bite. I'm trying to be on my best behavior considering everything that has just happened.

"YEAH!"

I nearly lose my wig as the whole damn stadium, including Nahlia, shouts together. The woman beside me springs to her feet and starts hopping like a rabbit on crack. The music flares. She shakes out of her brown coat and begins to sweat, making me think she is on some recreational drug. Her head drops, and

I see ghetto tracks that no innocent bystander should have to encounter. She swings her arm and narrowly misses my face.

Nahlia grabs my elbow and says, "Hold it together." I don't have to try much longer; the woman is out of breath thirty seconds after she starts. She falls back into her chair, sitting on her coat. As the music dies down, I finally realize the actual length of the stage. One of the ministers on the pulpit was running across it and could barely make it to both sides before sitting down looking wet and winded. I guess I would be tired too if I just ran across a stage that is almost as long as a football field.

I begin to smell peppermint like every woman just snagged a piece from their pocketbooks and unwrapped it. The lights over the stage dim slightly. I am starting to feel a bit confused about whether or not this is a concert or church service. Everyone is jumping on their feet and clapping their hands when a reasonably young guy comes out wearing a designer suit. It's the T.V. preacher. He has broad shoulders and an athletic frame. With his shortcut and goatee, he reminds me of Stain.

He takes the microphone and says, "Good morning, church. God is good."

"All the time," the congregation says in unison.

"And, all the time…"

"God is good," all the people shout while whistling, hooting, and howling. I feel like it's mating season in the Amazon rainforest.

"Today, I'm going to waste no time jumping into the message. I'm going to begin by reading an excerpt from the book I introduced last week. In it the author scribes:"

> I was great and mighty. I was all things wonderful. I was perfect in every way. Then I lived. That life stalled my successes and scrambled my strength. Life surprised me with tears that followed smiles and screams that chased laughter like a rabid dog. My might was questioned, my greatness in doubt. I sit and wonder who can love me now.

I snatch my program that dropped to the floor when the ghetto track lady startled me. I look for his name. Oh, God. I unglue my eyes from the program and glance back at the preacher. I realize there is someone else he looks like too—Nahlia's father.

§§§§§

After service, Nahlia and I follow a lanky guy with stylish, multi-colored glasses down a long corridor to a set of large, wooden double doors. There is an elegant design etched into them that border the words "Administrative Offices." The young guy, who looks fresh out of high school, adjusts his glasses like somebody's grandpa. He digs in the inner pocket of his chic metallic blazer, taking out a badge and waving it over the keypad to unlock the door.

As we walk through, there is a well-furnished reception area, serving as the hub for three separate hallways. Each hallway is named and color-coded. Straight ahead is the blue Administrative Wing, to the left is the green Financial Wing, and to the right is the red Pastoral Wing. Since a security guard, looking like he should be working as a bodyguard for a high profile rapper, is at the entrance of the Financial Wing, I assume that's the only hall with people there.

"Ladies, right this way," he says, pointing to the right hallway. When we walk past the Pastor's office, he turns to us and says, "The pastor has a young son, so he made a playroom near his office." He looks at Nahlia. "Would you like to go in here and play while your mom talks with the Pastor?"

Nahlia doesn't even hesitate to answer, "Yes!"

I place my hand on her back and push her towards the playroom door. "How do you say 'yes' without seeing it," I say, knowing she is about to try to suck her teeth at me. "It would be funny if it were just an empty white room with padded walls. That would teach you."

Neither of them finds my words funny. Walking into the church I thought I did a pretty good job picking out some unwrinkled jeans and a black sheer blouse to go with my Chucks, but the way this guy is sizing me up, I feel like trash.

He opens the door for Nahlia, brushes past me, and opens the Pastor's office door. He directs me inside and says, "Have a seat. The Pastor will be with you, momentarily." He gets ready to walk away but must have remembered his basic manners. "Is there anything I can get you while you wait?"

"No, thank you. I'm just fine."

As the door shuts, I take time looking around the spacious office. The room is exceptionally contemporary. Everything in the office is red, brown or gold. On one wall hangs a large portrait of a man looking up, surrounded by a bunch of lions. On a mantle are trophies and plaques representing everything from pastoral appreciation to ping pong. Just behind his clear desk is a metal partition connected to the ceiling. There is a red lever on the wall that appears to operate it.

What would he have back there?

I walk over to get a better look and pass the desk before realizing someone else is in the room.

"That's my private area." His deep voice causes me to freeze like an icicle. I can't even pivot my body to face him. "I do not mean private in the sense of secretive. No, it is more like…personal. It is my office getaway."

I don't know what button he pushes, but the partition begins to open up. Beyond the barrier is a full area rug with the biggest flat screen I have ever seen. "Movies, video games, air hockey, ping pong, and foosball are all here. I used to say I would live here if I had a refrigerator and a bathroom, so when I added both of them, my wife ensured I was home every night."

I flash a fake smile.

Whatever he pushed to open the partition, he hit again to close it. "Now, I do not normally have meetings standing up, but if you would like to, that will be just fine with me. I'm only going to have to ask you to at least face me so I can know with whom I'm speaking." He walks behind me. I face him and shake his extended hand.

"I'm Pastor Clark."

"I'm Gloria Sanchez."

"Who in your family is Mexican?" he asks.

"What do you mean?"

"Your last name is Sanchez. How did—"

"Okay. Let me explain something to you. You can't assume that everyone with a Spanish-sounding name is Mexican. My mother was black, and she told me that my father was Puerto Rican. No, Mexican there."

"Well, wonderful. I see we are off to a great start," Pastor Clark says. "How about we have a seat?"

"I guess. I am kind of tired."

"So, did you enjoy service today?"

"Well," I say as he motions me toward the plush, onyx sofa, "I was a little late, but the sermon was fine."

He plops down in a full-grain, mahogany leather chair. "The former pastor would tell us guys that the 'best preacher is the one that draws from his own well.' I have taken that word of advice from him, and I only preach what I have lived."

"Correct me if I'm wrong, but your message was "How the Mighty Can Fall."

"That's right."

"So, you have fallen?"

"Can I call you Gloria?"

"Sure."

"Gloria, all have sinned and fall short of the glory of God, even the mighty. And, yes, even a pastor." After the pastor chuckles to himself, he coughs and crosses his legs. "If you do not mind, I would like to bypass some of the usual small talk. Is that okay with you?"

"Yes. I'm just glad you were willing to meet me."

"Well, you caught me on a good day. No meetings after church, which is out of the ordinary around here. So, I must say that when I received your note, I was more than curious. You sent me the book?"

"Well, I did send it. But it wasn't for you."

"Well, how did I receive it if it wasn't meant for me? It had my name on it."

"It was for your father."

"Are you talking about that man?" he says, pointing behind me.

I twist my neck to see a painting of this pastor—just older. "That's him. What happened to the picture?"

"Oh, just a little accident," he says, flashing a grin at me.

"An accident? There is only glass missing from around his face. That doesn't look like an accident to me."

"Gloria, how did you know my father?"

"No offense, but I would like to tell him if you don't mind." I pull up to the edge of the chair, preparing to leave.

"No. I would not mind at all if he were here."

"Well, where is he?"

"He's dead," he says with the sincerity of a serial killer. "We had that picture made just before his untimely death." I take one of the deepest breaths of my life, and everything comes out: tears, snot, everything.

"I know. Pastor Clark touched so many lives," he says, running to get me a tissue so I can catch all of it. I cry like a soiled baby. It's like whatever tears didn't fall in the truck when I was hugging the steering wheel made sure to fall now. As he dashes back with the tissue, he must have noticed my bruises. "What happened to your neck?"

Even if I wanted to respond, no words could form now. I swipe my hands through my hair to cover the discoloration blotched across my neck.

Realizing my unwillingness to speak, he moved on. "Well, since he isn't here, why don't you sit back and tell me what you would have said to him."

Between sobs, I manage to say, "You won't care."

"I most definitely do care. I owe one you for that book you sent me. It saved my marriage." He sits back in his chair and crosses his leg again. "Whatever you have to tell me, I'm here to listen."

I manage to dry my face off with a dozen tissues. "I have a nine-year-old daughter."

"That's wonderful. I have a nine-year-old son. Is she over in the playroom?"

"Yes." I sigh. "And your father is her father."

"Huh? Repeat that for me."

"Your father is my daughter's father," I say.

"Are you saying what I think you are saying?" he asks, looking at me as if he was trying to look at my eyes through my black Versace shades.

I point to the picture behind me. "That man is her father." His handsome, auburn face goes ugly with confusion. "I'm a stripper." I fidget with the damp tissue in my hand. "At least I was a stripper. About ten years ago, when I first started in this business, I was hired to dance privately for your father. Afterward, he said he wanted to care for me. He had something special about him. I didn't know he was a pastor at first. He was kind, and I trusted him. He just wanted sex. I never heard from him again. After that, I only slept with my manager, but that wasn't until after my daughter was already born."

"He never mentioned you or said I had a sister."

"What do you think he would say, 'Son, I slept with a stripper, and now you have a little sister.'"

"I guess, but how do I know what you are saying is factual?"

He looks like he is trying to hold back his emotions. "He had a scar that looked like the Star of David on his side from where a steel rod stabbed him. He had teeth falser than the breasts of most of the girls I used to work with." I put my hands on my mouth and say, "Oh, I'm sorry. Can I say 'breasts' in here?" He nods. "He even had back hair in the shape of—"

"Okay, that's enough." He looks at the portrait and shakes his fist, "Even in death…even in death I can't get rid of you."

"I'm sorry for coming. I didn't mean to—"

"No. You are fine. I needed to know this. Tell me why you wanted him to know. Are you looking for money?"

I shake my head and say, "I wasn't until yesterday."

"Well, what made you send the book? It arrived two weeks ago."

"Nahlia's birthday is coming up soon, and I wanted her to know her real father. I wasn't trying to cause trouble. I just thought the book might help him have the right attitude to accept her back into his life."

"Okay," he sighs. "I did say I owed you for saving my marriage. I just need you to take off your hat and glasses first."

"I can't do that," I say, grabbing the brim of my hat and pulling it down further.

"Gloria, if you want help from me, I need you to do one simple thing: take off your glasses and hat."

"Oh, so you're like your old man, huh? You want me to strip for you too? I'm out of here." I grab my Burberry handbag and stand.

"No," he says, standing with his bottom lip quivering. "I am not my father. If I am going to help you, I need to know how much assistance you need."

I throw my shades and hat on the glass coffee table between us.

He doesn't flinch.

"You're pretty calm to see a woman that looks like the human fly."

"I'm a pastor. I have seen it all. Trust me." He pauses to get a better look at me. "These look pretty fresh. Have you been to the hospital?"

"Yes. I left there when they told me nothing was permanently damaged or broken."

"Okay. Can you tell me what happened?" he asks.

"It was a little accident, the same as that picture." We both laugh sweetly, allowing the short-lived carefree joy to clear out some tension.

"Is where you are staying safe?"

"My truck is the safest place I have right now. We were kicked out of my place, and all my money was stolen last night. Look, I don't want to bother you. Just let me get my daughter and get out of your hair."

"Sit down. I barely have any hair as it is so it would be quite a feat for you to get in it. Just let me call my wife. You and your daughter can stay in two of our guestrooms until you get back on your feet. Besides, my son, Oli, will love to have the company."

He walks over to his desk and searches for his phone. Finding it in the pocket of the coat hanging on his office chair, he dials his wife and puts the phone to his ear. "Hey, honey. I'm sorry to pull a Sabbath surprise on you, but we are going to have some company. I'll explain later, but could you get home and clean up our little mess in the dining room." He looks up at me and flashes a brilliantly, broad smile. Maybe Sundays aren't so bad after all.

§§§§§

CHAPTER 8: BRAYDEN FOSTER

Sunrise Over the City

∞ ∞ ∞

The crisp morning air has no chance. Not against the foul musk of twelve sore athletes running uphill through the woods. The morning's silence doesn't appear to either.

"Come on! Pick up the pace you pansies," Coach Bridge shouts, as he rides his bike beside us. "Almost there. Not much further now."

Running always makes my brain race. I can't help but wish I could have run faster to catch the truck that sped away. Hearing my feet squish the dew-damp ground has me thinking about how much I cried these last two weeks.

I've never been a crybaby, but I can't help it. What's good is that with all the sweat on my face, no one can tell I'm crying now. I've never wanted to not be me so much in my life. I wish I didn't like guys. I want to change this part of me that has my father despising me. If I can't be loved for being me, I'll settle for being what's expected from me.

"Hey, Foster, watch out man," Derek Moore says, pushing me away after I sidestep onto his foot.

"Sorry, dude."

"Foster, get it together," Coach shouts. "You're over there in la-la land. Is it too early for ya?"

"No, Coach."

"Well, wake up then!"

"Yes, Coach."

As we clear the trees, we reach a spacious opening near a vast lake. The sun is just beginning to peek over the horizon, casting a cascade of radiant colors across the sky. "Alright, ladies, time to turn around and run back to the school." The other four freshman recruits suck their teeth so loud it sounds like they had popcorn stuck in there. Coach laughs and turns his bike around. "Whoever can beat me back to the school doesn't have to run next week."

Everyone cheers—everyone but me. I'm too busy peering up as red and blue clash for space in the sky. I have always been captivated by the simplistic intricacy of a sunrise—the mixture of colors, the gradual brightening of the atmosphere, and disappearing stars.

"Foster, are you coming?" Jakes asks.

"Yea," I say without looking back. I can hear the sound of footsteps galloping away from me. I would join everyone, but nothing in me wants to be here. I breathe in deep, allowing the air to cool my nose hairs, but secretly wishing it could numb the parts in me that hurt.

"Newbie," I turn my neck and see Jakes still standing behind me, "what's going on with you, man?"

"I was just thinking," I say, knowing he can't see my tear trails through my sweat.

"What are you thinking about?"

"Well, I was thinking that with every sunrise there is a new beginning."

"Yeah. You're right. That's kinda deep." He takes a step forward, punching my left arm. "Has your dad called back yet?"

I exhale. "No."

"You never told me what you did to make him so mad," he says, as he positions himself beside me.

"Jakes, it's not what I did. It's what I told him. It shouldn't matter. I'm his only child, and he has been ignoring my calls for two weeks now. I don't deserve that."

"Whatever you did or said, it couldn't be that bad." He leans over and grips my sweaty shoulder. Something in my core reverberates. "Look, I know you two aren't speaking right now, but I'm sure he loves you."

"He doesn't love me," I say, trying to reclaim my focus. "He hates me." I swat his hand away as I turn to face the lake again.

"And?" Jakes asks.

"And what?"

"And, if he doesn't love you, are you going to lose your focus, your scholarship, and a chance to play for a professional team one day?"

I don't answer. Part of me is just being difficult. The other part doesn't know the answer.

"I'll take that as a 'no.' Foster, you're a great ballplayer, but you've got to get your head back in the game, or you won't have a team to play for." I hesitate, but, knowing he's right, I pivot towards him. "That's more like it. I'll race you back." His morning breath is like celestial glory to my primitive nostrils.

"Please, Jakes. You're too slow for me. I'd be finished with my shower before you even got halfway back."

"Oh really," Jakes says. "Since you're so confident, let's bet on it."

"What do you want to bet?" I ask.

"Loser has to be the other's errand boy for a week."

"Make it two, and I'm game," I say.

"Wow, you really are sure about your speed. For your sake, I hope you aren't letting your mouth get you in something you can't back up." I just raise my eyebrows and shrug my shoulders. Either way, I win. If I lose, I'm his for two weeks. If I win, he's mine. That just gave me my second wind.

"May the best man win," I say, shaking his firm hand.

§§§§§

"Um…you two must be in the wrong training camp," Coach says as we run through the gym doors, five minutes behind everyone else. "The cheerleading team's training is next door." Most of our teammates start laughing. "Hey, what's so funny?" Coach asks, turning to instruct the team again as if we never walked in.

Jakes motions for me to walk over with him to the bleachers where the rest of the team is resting. His face says he's unmoved by Coach's words, but his lurking feet say just the opposite. Even though I follow him, everything in me is hesitant about going near Coach. As we get halfway to the bleachers, Jakes stops dead in his tracks as Coach snaps his neck and glares at him. I stay hidden behind Jakes.

"Excuse me. What are you doing, Heart?" Coach asks.

"I was coming to sit down with the team," Jakes says, folding his arms.

"What part of what I said was unclear?"

"I just thought—" Jakes begins to say.

"You thought?" Coach sounds like the Joker, laughing at whatever killer punchline was in his head. All the black students—and some of the white kids that took African American Literature, affirming their "wokeness"—say coach looks like Countee Cullen in the face. That's debatable. What's undeniable is his short, soul brother afro that has a receding starting line, exposing every wrinkle and crease in his forehead as he laughs uncomfortably. He gains my father's respect for his racial barrier-breaking achievements on campus and in Charlotte. "Thinking is reserved for athletes, not cheerleaders. You should save your mental energy and go next door to your practice."

"Coach, I am—"

"Coach? I'm not your coach. Your coach is Ms. Riddick next door. I only coach men, not some little fairies that couldn't flap their wings fast enough to keep up with the group. No! My team can run to the lake and back in no more than an hour, not an hour and twenty minutes."

"Coach, it was my fault," I say, stepping around Jakes. "Heart was just being—"

"Just being what?" Coach asks. "Was he helping you find your manhood, Foster? Is that what you two were doing in the woods? Heart was helping you find out how to be a man?"

"No, Coach," I say, feeling like everyone knows my secret. It's hard to listen to a man who advocated for the rights of African Americans speak like such an ignorant, bigot. How is it possible for someone to be a respectable activist and still carry a disgraceful approach to handling marginalized people with a different issue than him? I'm supposed to admire him. But how do you respect a bully?

By now, all of the teammates are laughing hysterically. "Heart, maybe you should start doing twenty-minute training sessions for little fairies like Foster to become real men, since you're such a professional now." Out of the corner of my eye, I see Jakes lower his head.

"Coach, can we rerun it?" I ask.

"Of course you're going to rerun it. You know how you get to play in a Super Bowl?" he asks, expecting us to know the rehearsed answer. "Practice. So this time, I expect you two back in forty minutes. Anything less and you'll be running all day until you get it right. Got me?"

"Yeah," I say, dreading the thought of rerunning those five miles. Jakes doesn't say anything, so I nudge him with my elbow.

Jakes swivels his head and looks at me. Seeing how desperate I am to end this spectacle, he turns back to Coach and says, "Okay."

"Great!" Coach says. "Looks like you two cheerleaders might make it off the sidelines and into the game. I only have one question: Why am I still looking at you?" We shrug. "What do you need me to shoot a gun in the air?" He pulls out his stopwatch and hits the 'start' button. "You might want to start running now." We both dash to the green metal door, disappearing just after Coach turns back to the other teammates and says, "So, any other faggots in here?"

§§§§§

After sprinting to the lake and back, we stop to check in with Coach and hobble back to our dorm rooms. I can't stop thinking about how silently we ran. The only noise we made was the ground squishing under our feet and our heavy panting on the way back to the gym. We made a rhythm in our running that I fear will be difficult to recreate in our friendship now. My earlier victory of beating him back to the gym seems irrelevant after Coach's words.

We part ways without a word. I walk into my room and head straight for the shower. I'm nervous about what could happen at the next practice. Will Coach keep taunting me because I like guys? How does he even know? Did he talk with my father?

The steam that's filling the bathroom feels as thick as the mist of confusion in my heart. I just moved here, and I don't know anyone. Jakes is the only guy on the team I made a connection with.

What if the whole team knows? And, if they do, why is Jakes still willing to hang out with me? Does he have an ulterior motive? Does he like me more than a friend?

My life feels like a pane of thin glass with a brick going through it. Helpless, I don't know what to do at this point. I'm struggling in all the areas of my life that are important to me: sports, family, and school. Life shouldn't be this hard. It shouldn't hurt this much. I stand under the stream of hot water, wishing I could wash away my fear, my pain. Knowing no water can cure this, I try to clear my mind before turning the nozzle, stepping out of the shower and drying off.

I finish putting on some lounge pants and an old t-shirt when there is a knock at the door. I open it, discovering Jakes on the other side. "Hey, Foster," he says. "I see you took a shower too. Gotta wash that funk off, right bro?" I nod my head and look away. "What's wrong with you, man?" he asks, pushing into my room.

"I just feel horrible about today," I say.

He walks over to the plush chair in the far corner, saying, "Yeah, me too. I haven't had to run that much since I was a freshman."

"I'm sorry about that, Jakes."

"Newbie, you're going to have to learn to brush some stuff off, especially if you're going to deal with Coach."

"I know," I say, plopping down on the bed. "But, it's the other stuff Coach said too."

"What did he say?" Jakes asks.

"When we were running out he called me a faggot."

"He called us faggots," Jakes says. "And?" I shrug. "Again, that's just Coach being Coach. When he gets all riled up he says whatever he wants to say."

"But, it's like he knew."

"Knew what?"

"Everyone knows, don't they?" I ask, slipping off the bed and wandering around the room like I'm looking for something.

"Everyone knows what?"

"I know everyone knows I like guys," I shout.

"No. Everyone doesn't know, but, as loud as you just said that, I'm sure they know now." Jakes laughs to himself.

"Did you know?" I ask Jakes without looking at him.

"Yeah, I knew." My paralyzed face must give Jakes the impression I'm about to have a stroke because he stands up with concern in his eyes. "Are you okay, man?"

"I...ugh...how did you know?"

"Come on, Foster. I knew from day one. The way you were looking at me. The way you were talking to me—stuttering and everything. I knew."

"So, why are you still my friend?" I ask.

"My little brother liked guys," Jakes says, sitting back on the bed. "So, when Coach paired us up, I just figured it was fate."

"He did like dudes? He doesn't like them anymore?"

"Well, actually, he died about two years ago." His head drops so hard it nearly falls in his lap.

"I'm so sorry to hear that," I say, freezing my roaming of the room.

"Thanks, man," he says, shaking his head. "Well, life happens in ways we never expect."

"If you don't mind me asking, how did he die?"

"His name was Spencer, but I called him 'Spinna,' because he could take anything—clothes, a dance, anything—and put his spin on it." Jakes goes silent. Without uttering a word, he looks up and bites his lip. He squeezes his eyes shut and exhales.

"My brother wasn't exactly quiet about his preference. When we were growing up, he would get picked on all the time, and I would be there to stand up for him. But…" For the first time, I see Jakes cry. He's wiping his tears away like they're burning his face. "Sorry, I guess I'm still not all the way over it."

"It's okay, Jakes. I don't think you ever get all the way over something like that." I take a step back and perch on my thick Maplewood desk. My feet dangle off the edge like kids in a chair waiting for their parents to pick them up from school.

"I guess you're right," he says, without looking up. "One day, I wasn't there for him. Two guys took him to a cornfield and nearly beat him to death. They left him there to suffer all night. I searched all night for him, but I couldn't find him. The next morning, a woman calls me on Spinna's phone, telling me he's at the hospital. He didn't live much longer. Right before he died, he said, 'I just want you to remember I lived.' I insisted the school retire his basketball number, even though he was a freshman."

"Wow. That's awesome that you did that for him, dude," I say, transfixed by Jakes' sensitivity.

"Yeah, alright. Enough of this mushy stuff." Finally, he erects his back, lifts his head, and stares at me. His fiery eyes held a sincerity I only glimpsed when he took me to my room after my father abandoned me. "It's like this, Brayden. You remind me of my brother. You're not feminine or nothing, but you're a cool guy like he was. I know you're pretty much alone, so I would appreciate it if you let me look out for you."

"Sure," I say, trying not to sound like I'm a woman reacting to him proposing.

"Cool. So, what are you doing tonight?"

I pick up the cellphone on the desk. "I have a date."

"A date?"

"Just a guy I met online."

"Don't tell me you're one of those people who get hookups online," he says, looking disgusted.

"Hey, don't judge me."

"I'm not judging you. I don't see the point of trying to find love on an app."

"I'm not expecting to find my soul mate. But I don't know anyone here. Even if I make a friend that would be cool."

"Well, where are you two going?" Jakes asked, sounding more like my father.

"There is this club downtown that I wanted to try out. I've never been out with a guy before, so this is all new to me. I figure that I might as well try it out while I'm young. Since you're giving me this feeling like you're my dad, I do have a favor to ask."

He starts laughing. "What is it, Foster?

"Will you drop me off at the club?"

"Sure. I have a party to go to myself. I'll drop you off on the way."

"Ah, man. Thanks so much."

"No prob. Let me go crash for a minute so I can be right for tonight. Alright lil' bro, I'll hit you up in a few."

As he turns and walks out of my room, I can't help but feel like I'm not an only child anymore.

§§§§§

After driving across town, we finally arrive at the club, Scorpios, in Jakes' Midnight Blue Mustang. The club is as big as a Greek Coliseum, built like a warehouse at the bottom of a steep hill. As we drive down, the rumble of the engine attracts more attention than desired.

"Can't you keep this thing quiet," I say to Jakes.

He looks and me and laughs. "This is a man's car, bro. It's going to make a little noise. Now, get out and go have fun." As I open the door, he grabs my shoulder and says, "Be careful. Okay?"

"Of course, I will." I stand up and shut the door.

"Call me if you need me," Jakes says, shifting the car in reverse.

"Will do." I salute him as he turns the car around and speeds up the hill—all while honking his horn.

The guy I'm supposed to be meeting, Robert, told me he was standing in line when I called him a few minutes ago. I assumed finding him was going to be easy, but this crowd is wrapping around the building. I begin to search the line from back to front, using my memory of Robert's profile picture. I decided to move closer.

I was almost finished searching the line when a guy calls out my name: "Hey, Brayden." I turn around and look, but I don't see anyone who looks like the profile picture. "Brayden!"

"Yes?" I refuse to take one step towards him, even though he is about 20 feet away.

"I'm Robert," he says, waving me over. Now every part of me is in disbelief. He made his profile seem like he woke up in Chris Brown's body, but he looks more like Danny Devito. He said he had an athletic build, but the only thing athletic he does is watch sports on T.V.

"You're Robert?" I ask, sounding like I know this is a practical joke.

"Yeah, I'm Robert." I didn't mean to be rude, but I'm waiting for Jakes to pull up any minute laughing. I decide to squash his joke before he can get me. "So, where is your hair, Robert?" I ask, pointing at his bald head. "In your pic you have hair."

"Oh, that's an old picture," he says, looking a bit uneasy. "So, you've never been here before, right?"

"Nope. I've never been here before. Look, Robert, can I be honest with you?"

"Sure," he says.

"You look nothing—"

"I look nothing like my profile. I know. I just hoped someone would go out with me. I don't get many offers to go on dates with my real picture and stats."

"But you lied, dude," I say, as I twist my head away from him. "That's not cool. I would have rather gone out with someone honest that I may not be attracted to than an attractive liar. Just be you. So, while I wanted to go to this club tonight, I just don't feel right going in now. Enjoy your night."

"Are you sure I—"

"Robert, I'm sure that tonight you don't want me as a date, and I don't want my first date with a guy to start with a lie. Enjoy your night."

I turn and walk towards the hill.

"Hey, where are you going sexy?" a random dude asks.

I must admit. I've been attractive most of my life. With my smooth hazelnut skin, chiseled body, and sharp features, men and women have wanted me. But, I've never had someone grab my arm and call me sexy.

"I have to go," I say.

"Stay. I want to dance with you." It's clear he had a few drinks before arriving. I'm in not in the mood to deal with someone drunk.

"Stay? What am I? A dog? I have to go," I say, as I head towards the hill.

"Your loss," he shouts.

"Well, I don't mind losing sometimes."

When I reach the street at the top of the hill, I try to call Jakes several times to have him come pick me up, but he's not answering. I stand there for about twenty minutes, considering calling a taxi when a black Expedition pulls in front of me with two of my senior teammates—Terrance and Dan—calling for me.

Terrance, the Hornet's center, is built like Shaq with tree-trunk sized arms covered in tattoos. Running into him on the court is like riding a bike into a tractor-trailer. He's the darkest guy on the team, so they nicknamed him 'Midnight.' At just over six feet, Dan is the team's point guard. He looks bleached white, so they call him 'Ghost.' People call them 'Ebony and Ivory' since they are best friends and rarely seen without the other.

"What you doing here, man?" Dan asks.

"Oh...I...I'm just trying to get Jakes to pick me up."

"Dawg, whatcha doing out here?" Terrance demands. "Why, you in front of that sissy spot?" I stand there in silence like Medusa's glare turned me to stone. What am I supposed to say? I'm barely past my second week here, and already two of my teammates are catching me in spots that could ruin my reputation on campus. They must take my hesitation as an answer. They look at each other and smile.

"It's all good man," Dan says, reassuringly. "Hop in. We'll take you back to campus."

I get in the back seat and buckle up. I try to pay attention to the road, but the music is so loud I can barely concentrate. Jakes still hasn't responded to any of my texts. I send a short message letting him know I'm okay. This city is still a mystery to me, but, looking back at the road, something isn't right. It's taking too long to get back to campus. We get on this road that is long and dark. The only light around is coming from the truck's headlights.

"Guys, where are we going?" I have to scream to ask.

"Huh?" Dan shouts back.

"Where are we going?"

"Oh, we need to make a quick stop." I fall back into the cloth seat and lean my head on the window. I notice we are approaching a large field. I try to call Jakes again, but I have no signal out here.

We stop.

Terrance cuts the car off, saying, "We're here."

"Where is here?" I ask.

"It's a freshman surprise," Dan says, getting out of the car. Both of them walk to the trunk and rummage around. After they grab whatever they were looking for, they walk to opposite ends of the truck, opening the backseat doors.

"Get out!" Terrance barks.

"What's going on, guys?" I ask.

"Look, Brayden," Dan says. "I would do what Terrance says. You don't want to make him angry."

"Okay, just tell me what's going on," I say.

"This is your freshman orientation," Dan says, as friendly as on my first day of practice. Afraid of Terrance, I start to get out on Dan's side. When my feet touch the dirt ground, Dan shuts my door.

"Are you leaving me out here?" I ask.

"Yep," Dan says.

"I have to get home on my own?"

"If you can walk," Dan says while grinning.

"If I can—" Terrance smashes a wooden bat against my side.

"Yeah, faggot. If you can walk." Terrance says, sounding like a hyena as I roll on the ground gripping my hip. Dan doesn't resort to weapons. He kicks me while Terrance swings at me like he's trying to hit a home run. After a few moments, Terrance seems to get bored with the bat. He tosses it to the ground and walks back to the trunk. He comes over with a gas canister.

"You wanna be a lil' flaming sissy. I'm about to show you what a real flame is."

Dan looks at what Terrance is doing and says, "No man. We can't do that."

Terrance glares at Dan, who doesn't blink once. "Okay, fine." He looks over at me and growls, "You better be lucky Dan doesn't want to smell your faggoty flesh burn." He starts beating me so hard I begin to pray for death.

At that moment, I think of Spencer, and how Jakes will feel knowing this has happened. All my thoughts shatter as they strip me naked. I'm so weak that my body is unable to fight back. I'm barely able to move. They flip me like a pancake onto my stomach, knocking the air from my lungs. Soon, I feel hands on my back. The torture happening behind me is so painful my body twitches. I scream silently, wishing someone could rescue me from the terror attack on my body. It feels like a chunk of my soul is being ripped from within. In that field, on my stomach, barely able to move, my first male sexual experience is rape.

I just want someone to know I lived. This is my last thought before I blackout.

The sound of a woman shrieking awakens me to her horror show. It doesn't take me long to know that this is no dream. "Call the ambulance! Call the ambulance!" Her scream is the result of my naked, battered flesh covered in blood.

What seems like hours pass before I hear the sound of the ambulance, approaching. When the paramedics arrive, since I am still lying on my stomach, they prep me so they can roll me onto the stretcher. Everything I touch feels like a spear piercing me. When they finally strap me on the gurney, I open my eyes for the first time that day. I realize it's sunrise.

Chapter 9: Oliver Clark, Jr.

Family First

∞ ∞ ∞

A week later and today almost feels like a typical Sunday.

"Is Rachel done with that food yet?" Terry asks, dipping his tortilla chip into the bowl of homemade salsa on my living room table.

"Terry, you ask me the same thing every Sunday," I say.

"How many times have you preached that we should pray without ceasing?" Terry asks.

"More times than you probably heard."

"Oh, you have jokes today," Terry says, holding his chip like a dainty British woman.

"You don't think I am naturally funny?" I ask, watching him devour the nacho with ease.

"Junior, stop playing. You're going to make me choke over here."

"Terry, you can choke on that chip if you want to. I'm a preacher, not a doctor. I am sure Rachel will call us when the food is ready, as always."

Terry has remained a faithful friend for nearly three decades. He grew up next door to my family, in one of the three houses on our cul-de-sac. While he doesn't know his biological parents, his adopted family is awe-inspiring. After abusive sessions with my father, I would sneak to Terry's house and play with his action figures until it got dark. My father never noticed. He was too preoccupied in his offices at home or church. After my mother passed, he didn't care to be in my presence for too long. So, being at Terry's was better than being home alone or sitting in that boring church.

"Are we adding two more to the table?" Terry asks.

"You know, for someone who eats over here every week and doesn't have to cook or clean, you sure are concerned about who is at the table. If I didn't know any better, I would think you were making a guest list."

"Junior, why do you want to mess with me when I'm hungry?" he asks, scooping up a handful of chips in his brawny hands.

"I just thought I would add to what is already being done on the television," I say.

"What's that?"

"Your team is getting whooped by the Steelers, and I know that's messing with you," I say pointing to my championship ring.

"Why can't we ever just watch one football game without you pointing to that Cracker Jack ring?" Terry asks.

"Don't get mad at me for being a winner," I say, waving the ring around.

"You won at fantasy football, not an actual game. Besides, when was the last time you held a real football?"

"Umm…well…I—," I mutter.

"Exactly!"

I grab the remote and turn the volume up to drown out his voice. "And, I am still a winner," I shout, facing the television.

Terry snatches the remote out of my hand, and I watch as the volume bar on the television slides down. "Junior," he says, with a pensively, baritone voice. "What are you going to do?"

"Well, I want to upgrade the surround sound in here to be able to—" I begin.

"No," Terry says, leaning forward. "I'm talking about with everything going on in your life: your father dying, you drinking again, and this woman and her kid in your house. What are you going to do?"

"You want an answer to all of that? That is a lot to address."

"Hell, yeah," Terry says. "You have a lot going on right now, sir. Just talk to me. What's going on? What's your game plan here?"

"I wish I had a concise answer for you. I don't. I'm just trusting that God has a better answer for you than I do."

"I hear you, but what's up with them staying here anyway?" Terry asks. "How do you know them?"

"Oliver, dear, can you come here for a moment?" Rachel asks, stepping into the doorway of the living room.

"Sure, honey," I say as I stand. "Excuse me for a minute, Terry."

"No problem," Terry says, grabbing the remote to turn back up the volume.

When I walk into the hallway, Rachel begins to walk towards my study. She enters and holds the door open for me, closing it behind me once I pass the threshold. With her left hand still on the doorknob, she asks, "Are you okay?"

"Yeah, I would say I'm fine."

"That's good, but I'm not," she says, releasing the door handle to grasp my hands.

"Rachel, what's wrong?"

"To start, there is a strange woman and her child living in our house. It's been a week. You know I don't mind helping people out, but this situation is just too much for me. I want you to be honest with me."

"Of course, I will," I say, squeezing her hand.

"Is that child yours?" she asks. Her eyes begin to swell up with tears.

"Honey, I told you the truth about this. Thank you for being so understanding. I realize that these last few weeks have been challenging for you. It isn't any easier for me. How do you think I feel knowing I have a sister by a woman who is a stripper? You know me better than this. What is really on your mind?"

"I got a phone call from Mrs. DuBois," she says, lowering her head. "She and Deacon are planning on coming over here after dinner."

"Why?"

"She didn't flat out say that she knew about Gloria, but she mentioned a matter of grave concern for the church." I cannot help but sigh as I rub my forehead. "What are we going to do?"

"I'm not sure just yet," I say.

"I heard you in there talking to Terry. Even he is asking questions," she says, waving her arms around like an aircraft marshal on a runway. "You are going to have to get some answers quickly. People are people." She moves towards the window, pulling back the scarlet Victorian country curtains to peer out to the cul-de-sac. "They are going to inquire and investigate why the pastor of one of the largest and most historic churches in the city has a stripper and her daughter staying with him."

"There are so many things going through my head right now that it is hard to settle on one answer," I say, feeling a headache approaching like a raging bull.

"Well, I will support you, but let me offer a word of advice." Rachel may be short but—when convicted by a thought or feeling—her hips spread like butter. She finds hidden curves to rest her hands on while sharing her opinion. At present, she drops the curtain back to its original position. Rachel paces towards me while pressing her French manicured hands into the sides where her violet sequined lace bodice meets her chiffon skirt.

"While you may not have cared about your father," she begins, "the church, community, and other clergy did. His funeral was televised. So, you're going to have to decide whether you want him remembered for being an advocate for civil rights and other social justice issues, locally and worldwide, or as another leader that couldn't keep it in his pants. Whatever path you choose, I'm here. Just know I would sleep easier knowing that the statue the city wants to build of him would represent his service instead of his scars."

She leans over and soothes my soul by caressing my lips with hers. "Thank you," I say, grabbing the sides of her stunning face to draw her in again. After she pulls back her warm lips from mine, Rachel dawdles from my side, slowly closing the office door as she exits from the room. I'm left in silence, with only the sound of my thoughts racing.

§§§§§

When dinner ended, so did Terry's presence at the house.

"Terry always eats like a bear headed into hibernation," Rachel says, laughing at how many aluminum foil-covered plates he took with him in a plastic grocery bag.

"Well, he does look like a bear and works out almost every day, so he keeps a pretty healthy appetite. I'm just glad he got along with Gloria and Nahlia at dinner."

"What did you tell him about them?" Rachel asks, handing me another plate to load into the dishwasher.

"I just mentioned that they are family and needed help. He didn't press the issue from there."

"That was honest and yet obscure. I'm proud of you honey," she says, giving me a fist bump. "You're getting better at being politically correct."

Ding-dong!

"Honey," Rachel says, "close the dishwasher. I think the DuBoises are here."

"We just talked them up," I say, shutting and starting the machine.

"Why would you say that?" she asks as she heads towards the front door.

"We were just talking about animals, right?" We snicker like school kids sneaking to tell an inappropriate joke.

Rachel shakes her head. "Oliver, I am not fooling with you tonight." She stops near the door and looks back at me. "I need you to be on your best behavior."

"I have known Deacon DuBois all of my life. The old man is pretty harmless. Besides, I am well equipped to handle him. Let's open the door and get this over with."

"Best behavior…" Rachel's voice trails off as she opens the door. "Hello there! How are you, Deacon and Mrs. DuBois?"

"We're just fine," Deacon DuBois says, barging through the doorway.

"Yes," Mrs. DuBois says, "we are. It's just mighty cold out there for early October."

Rachel walks behind Mrs. DuBois and says, "I agree. Why don't you let me take your coat?"

"Why thank you, Mrs. Clark," Mrs. DuBois responds.

My wife continues to play the ever-happy hostess. "Not a problem at all," she says. "Why don't you follow me into our living room and leave the boys to talk?"

"Why that sounds most agreeable to me," Mrs. DuBois replies. "Just show me the way." As they disappear around the corner, I am contemplating my next course of action. Ernest Lee told me to love above all else.

Before I can commence with Ernest Lee's decree, Deacon DuBois says, "My coat, here it is."

"Thank you, Deacon." I take his black overcoat and throw it over my arm.

"Just call me Archie tonight. Let's put aside our titles for now if that's okay with you."

"I'll agree to that," I say, pointing to the study to my right. "Let's have a seat in my study." When I walk into the room, I hang Archie's coat on the coat rack and head for my chair. As we take our seats, I ask, "To what do I owe the distinct pleasure of your presence in my humble abode?"

"Save the stunts son," Archie says, leaning forward. "My refrigerator is older than you."

"That is a shame," I say with an unrelenting smile. "What's your point?"

"I wasn't finished." He sits back and crosses his legs. "You and I don't get along. Honestly, I don't like you. I never liked you, but you were your father's son. That provided you at least a small portion of my attention. However, your father—God rest his soul—is dead. And, now, so are you."

"You come to my house with this brazen attack on—"

"Once again, I'm not finished." Archie smirks as he revels in the thought of silencing me. "You're nothing like your father. He was calculated and wise; you are emotional and muddle-headed. You should have appreciated him more. Maybe some of his positive traits would have rubbed off on you."

"I don't need a lecture on my father!" I say, pointing my finger so hard I think it will shoot a bullet.

"You just proved my point." While I can hear the cruel nature in his calm tone, it is his brusque countenance that reveals his engrained callousness. "My ultimate goal is to see your name removed from anything having to do with Greater Mount Pleasant Baptist Church. Whether it is with you walking away or being dragged away, my days will be spent removing you from office. Now, you may ask why I would come to your house and be so blunt about my intentions, but you have made this incredibly easy for me."

"Do tell, Archie," I say, placing my elbows on my desk.

"Well, your mental stability has been a hot topic of debate recently. I know the death of your father had a significant effect on you. Your violent outburst towards your father's portrait reflects that. Now, you're bringing in strippers off of the street to live with you in your father's old house. I don't know your relation to this woman and her child, but I will know soon enough.

"That woman and her—"

"No. No. No," Deacon says, "I don't need your explanation. Whatever I find out, I'm sure it won't be good for you."

"Why are you so adamant against me being the pastor?" I ask, startled by his viscous candor.

"It's not you, per se. It's the thought of you. I know you have secrets, young man. We need a leader, not a liability. Whatever skeletons you have, consider me your gravedigger, because I will find them."

He stands.

"No need to join me in standing. I know where to find my coat, and I'm more than familiar with the exit. I'll get my wife and be going." He takes a handful of steps towards the door before facing me again. "On a brighter note, I have been impressed with your sermons these last two Sundays. You seem…inspired." He grabs his coat and arranges it over his forearm. Before he shuts the door behind him, he glances at me one last time and smirks. "Goodnight, Pastor."

UNLOVABLE

§§§§§

I cannot bear to walk back out of my study to say 'goodbye'. With my head pounding, I reach for a small bottle of aspirin in my lower desk drawer. *This is the perfect time for a drink.* Tremors pulse through my anxious left hand as it reaches for a half-empty bottle of gin and places it on the desk. The sincerest part of me knows that I can cure these shakes with a few sips. The fiery, clear liquid always invades me with numbness that never fails.

Conviction is like a guard dog barking at the liquor burglar trying to break into my salivating mouth. The last time my hand touched a bottle, it also struck my wife. What would Terry say if he saw me now? What would Rachel think?

The front door closes, and I hear my wife's footsteps approaching my study. She walks in without knocking and sees the bottle of gin, just as I try to hide it under the bureau. "What's that, Oliver?"

"Umm…it is—it's not what you think."

"What should I think?" She crosses her arms over her chest, locking them in like an infinity sign. "Should I think you left me alone with Deacon and his wife so you could get a drink?" Her long, black twists fall from her ample shoulders, resting on her back as she looks at the ceiling. "What is that bottle even doing in here? I thought you threw them all out," she says, lowering her head to stare at me like a stranger.

"I…I…was—"

"Oliver Rustin Clark, I can't believe you. You promised me. You said you would never go back. What about me? What about your son?"

"Honey—" I begin.

"There's no honey here, Oliver," she says, clapping her hands with each word like a drunken hoodrat about to fight someone on a street corner. "I'm taking Oli, and we are going to my mother's house. You can stay here and drink yourself stupid, but we won't be around to deal with this foolishness tonight. You left me, Oliver. I had to sit with that DuBois woman and…" her voice trails off as she walks back out of the room, slamming the door behind her. "Oli!"

CHAPTER 10: GLORIA SANCHEZ

The Dark Night

∞ ∞ ∞

"Oli!"

Through the smokescreen of sleep that these pain meds have me in, I can hear Mrs. Clark shouting. After the sound of a door slamming, I can't help but think she might be in real trouble. I slide out of my quilted bed and stagger to the bedroom door.

"Oli!" Mrs. Clark's screams sound closer this time.

I open the door. Trying to keep from yawning, I poke my head through the doorway. Mrs. Clark is screaming alright, but she looks like her feet were frozen halfway up the stairs. "Are you alright, Mrs. Clark?"

"I'm just fine, Gloria. Thank you," she says like she is looking straight through me. "Oli!"

"I can go get him, Mrs. Clark." I have no clue what is happening right now, but I know better than to mess with a woman when she is on a mission.

I dash three doors down the hallway to Oli's room. Caught up in the excitement of the moment, I spring open his door. Oli's eyes jump to me and then back to his T.V. screen. "Your mother is out here about to blow out a lung calling for you. Why is that T.V. so loud? No wonder you can't hear your mother shouting your name. What are you doing?"

"Oh, I'm playing video games," Oli says, shaking both his hands while gripping the game controller with no sign of stopping.

"Well, you need to come on now. Your mother is out here about to—"

"I'm almost done," he says, without looking at me.

"Oli, I was sleeping. Your mother woke me up, calling out your name. Now, if I have to hear her say your name one more time, you're gonna wish you were in that video game with all those explosions."

He looks up at me.

"Oli, now!" Mrs. Clark yells from the staircase.

Before the sound of her voice trails away, I turn the T.V. off, pick up the game console, and unplug every cord connected to it. "Here," I say, handing him back the console. "You need to listen the first time your mother calls you. Now, get out there." He looks at me like I just ate his birthday cake. "Go on now."

He jumps to his feet and sprints down the hall. "I'm coming, Mom," he says.

As I walk back down the hall, I hear Mrs. Clark tell Oli, "Go and grab some clothes."

"Where are we going?" Oli asks.

"Oli—" Mrs. Clark begins as I take Oli's shoulder and turn him back towards his room.

I lean down to his ear and say, "This is the wrong time to ask questions and the right time to get your clothes together." I give him a gentle nudge to help him start walking back to his room. When I turn towards the staircase, I see Pastor Clark and Mrs. Clark staring at one another.

"Go back into your office, Oliver," Mrs. Clark says. "I don't even want to look at you right now."

"I'm not going anywhere, and neither are you," Pastor says, placing his foot on the bottom step. "You can't leave me, Rachel."

"What are you going to do? Are you going to hit me or slap me again? What?"

I'm sure neither of them notices my face contort with confusion. I expected just about anything to happen in the strip club, but how is the first lady getting slapped in the preacher's house?

"No, let me love you," Pastor says, taking another step up the staircase. "This is all a misunderstanding."

"You stop right there," Mrs. Clark says. "I've tried everything I know to make you realize that you don't know how to love me."

"What do you mean?" Pastor asks.

I duck behind the corner as Rachel looks down the hallway. "Oli, hurry up!" she says, turning back towards her husband. "Loving me is you not drinking. Loving me is being there for me when a disrespectful hag comes into our home and insults me as a woman and mother. Loving me is—"

Before Pastor Clark can take another step up the stairs, I race down the hall and poke my head into the bedroom next to Oli's. Nahlia is in bed, fast asleep. I swear that girl could sleep through the Super Bowl on the 50-yard line. I close the door and walk into Oli's room. "Are you about ready?" He nods his head without looking at me. "What you can't talk now?" He offers a half shrug and turns away from me to wipe his face.

He's crying.

"Stay in here until I come to get you okay." I don't wait for a reply. I back out of the room, shutting the door. I sprint to the top of the staircase.

"Yes, I do!" Mrs. Clark shouts.

"No, you don't," Pastor says. "You don't want a divorce. You love me."

"How can I love you when you don't even love yourself?" Mrs. Clark asks.

"You two need to stop now," I say.

"How can you say that?" Pastor says to his wife.

"People who love themselves know how to love others." Mrs. Clark says. "You're just a—"

"Now!" I shout, finally getting their attention. "You two are acting like children when you have two children up here. Your son is up here being traumatized because his mother and father don't know how to talk to one another when they are upset."

"Gloria, he—" Mrs. Clark begins, pointing to Pastor.

"I don't care what either of you did. This isn't the time or place. Mrs. Clark, if you want to leave, then just leave. All the dramatics aren't necessary. I swear you are just one dead dog away from a country song. And Pastor, it sounds like your wife has every right to go cool off. Now, I'm going to get Oli. It's time for you two to grow up," I say snapping my fingers. Shifting my eyes to each of them, I glare until I feel my words have gone deep like a sunken ship. Their mouths are so tight it looks like they sucked on a dozen lemons. "Good."

I walk back to Oli's room. When I open the door, I say, "Your mom is ready." He walks past me with a lowered head.

When he takes my spot at the top of the stairs, his mom looks up at him. "Oli, come on and say goodbye to your father." Rachel walks down the steps, brushes past her husband, and grabs her keys.

As Rachel steps to the front door, Oli drags his bag down the stairs and embraces his father. "Bye, dad."

"Goodbye, son. I love you."

"I love you too," Oli says, looking up at his father's eyes.

Pastor rolls his eyes toward his wife. "I am not going to let you take my son."

"Yes, I am," Rachel says, reaching for Oli's arm.

"Pastor," I say, "you need to let them go." He scowls at me, so I go down a few steps and fold my arms and return the favor. His hands slip from Oli's shoulders. He scans his wife.

"Come on, Oli," she says, pulling Oli towards her. Pastor's brown skin turns so red that I think he's about to erupt. Instead, he walks back into his study and slams the door like a professional wrestler.

Mrs. Clark opens the front door. "Oli, get situated in the car," she says. As Oli walks to the black raven Cadillac Escalade SUV, she looks up at me. "Thank you."

"I thought I was the one who was supposed to have all the issues. Look, you don't need to be thanking me. You need to be figuring out either how to be in love with him or how to be in love without him. I was with a man for almost ten years who had me stripping. He would sleep around, steal from me, and hit me if I said anything about it. He didn't really love me, but I stayed with him. I stayed because no matter how pretty I thought I was, I didn't love myself. Hold on one minute. Stay right there." I sprint back up the stairs to my room and grab my only book.

When I come down the stairs, she asks, "What's that?"

"It's a book you need to read. I've highlighted some parts. In fact, let me read this—"

"Gloria, I really need to be going."

"You're just running away. That can wait a minute." I clear my throat as I flip through the pages. "Ah, here it is. This is where he talks about thinking he was loved by darkness." I glance at her and shift back down at the book to read:

> When I thought I found love, love hadn't found me. Love was a distant and obscure mystery. In all of my days, I dare not say that love can be mastered, but it has surely mastered me. It drives me like a slave master. I need to love, need to be loved. It snaps my heart with a whip of loneliness in an attempt to keep me in my dark corner of isolation. It forces me to think, 'I'm not through with this corner yet. I still have trails for my tears to flow through. I still have more sorrow to sift. I still have more pain to process.' This darkness seems to be my friend. One day, I wake up in darkness, crying out in pain. I shout, 'Help me! Help me!' But, the darkness only taunts me, and that's when I realize darkness never loved me.

"Okay, so what does that mean, Gloria."

"It means that you should never fall in love with darkness."

"What darkness, dear?" Mrs. Clark asks.

"Darkness uses your pain or anger to trick you into rejecting true love. Darkness wants you to think it will console you, but its only true goal is to leave you lonely, bitter, and scared to love or be loved again."

I step closer to her. "Don't stop loving just because you don't feel loved. Feelings can change at any moment, and you would hate to make a permanent decision because of a feeling." I take her hand and put the book in it. She wraps her other arm around my neck, hugging me like the world was coming to an end.

"Thank you," she says with fresh tears flowing from her eyes.

"You're welcome."

She steps through the doorway, and I watch as she gets in the van. After shutting the door, I lock it. I start to walk to Pastor's office, but I have nothing to say. I head back up to bed. "Lord, help me to love above all else. Help me to love above all else."

§§§§§

Over two hours have passed, and I'm still awake. Going back to sleep is harder this time. Even my pain meds seem to have no effect. I'm left listening to the night's sounds. My heart is pounding in my chest like I just finished running up thirty flights of stairs. The crickets chirp so loud it sounds like they're barking. Maybe they're afraid of the dark like me. I feel silly being someone that worked at night and still being afraid of the dark, but I never got over what happened to me by my mom's boyfriend when I was a child.

"The Lord," I say, "is my shepherd, I shall not want. God makes me lie down in green pastures; God leads me to still waters. God restores my soul." Growing up, my mother would have me read this psalm at night. The version I read said, 'He' instead of 'God.' I can't bring myself to think of God as a man after knowing what men are capable of doing. It feels better to say 'God' anyways. "God guides me to paths of righteousness for God's name's sake."

My eyes open. Was that a floorboard creaking? Silence. I wait a few more moments and close my eyes again.

"Yea, though I walk through the valley of the shadow of death, I will fear no evil, for you are with me." There it is again. Through the darkness, I peer at the bedroom door, wishing I had X-ray vision. There is a low rumbling noise coming from somewhere in the upstairs hallway. I wish I could shut up those darn crickets.

"Your rod and staff, they comfort me." I hear another creaking sound, and I sit up. Part of me wants to feel safe here, but the other part wants to toss my feet over the edge of the bed and lock the door. I decide to investigate, so I slide my feet into my Burberry Cashmere slippers and glide towards the door.

When I place my ear to the wooden door, I hear what sounds like Pastor Clark's voice, but I can't make out his words. I can tell he is coming up the stairs, but I don't know what's taking him so long. Waiting for another five minutes, I can hear his feet shuffle across the wooden floor.

"You!" he shouts out, sounding like a ghost while banging his fist against my door. Startled, I jump back. I end up tripping over my feet and landing—not so gracefully—on my back. His hand turns the doorknob and opens the door. I see his frame in the doorway.

"What do you want?" I ask.

"I want to know why?"

"Why what?" I ask as I get back to my feet.

"Why are you doing this to me?" He takes a few steps staggering towards me.

"What did I do?" I ask, positioning myself at the side of the bed.

"You're working with her," he says. "I know you are."

"What are you talking about?"

"Don't try to play naïve," he says, moving towards the bed. "You're working together to get me back." With his slurred speech and the smell of gin on his lips, it is apparent that he's drunk.

"You're not okay right now," I say. "Go lay down. We can get your wife back in the morning."

"You lie!" he shouts. "Why are you trying to hurt me?"

"I'm not trying to—"

"I won't let you. I won't let you!" He hobbles towards me with his hands extended and moaning like a mummy.

"Stop!" I shout, jumping on and off the bed to land near the door. I face him and watch as he slowly turns his body back toward the doorway to pursue me.

"Come here," he says.

"Look," I say, walking backward, "I know you're drunk right now, but you don't want to do this with me tonight."

"Don't you tell me what I want," he says. "I tell you! And I want you and your bastard daughter outta my house."

"You don't mean that," I say, stepping into the hallway.

"Stop trying to tell me what you mean…I mean, what I mean." His shoulder hits the side of the door, and he nearly falls over.

"I can't take this," I say. "If you want me out, I'm out of here." I turn and head towards Nahlia's room.

"Where do you think you're going?" he asks.

"I'm going to get my daughter," I say, stopping to look back at him.

"No, you're going to get out now!" he shouts. I disregard him and turn towards my daughter's room. As I'm walking, I feel a hand gripping my shoulder. "I said now!"

"Let me go," I say swatting his hand away. He tries to grab me again, so I turn and push him away from me. He stumbles backward. In an attempt to regain his balance, he tries to catch hold of anything on the wall that will help. He finds nothing but the sound of glass shattering because his hand is knocking down the family portraits on the wall. "Watch out!" I shout as he nears the top of the stairs.

"Huh?" he mutters, just before he goes over the edge. His body bangs and crashes against the wall until he finally smacks against the last step.

"Oh, no!" I say. I dash to the top of the staircase, avoiding the glass, and see him sprawled across the ground—not moving.

"Mom, what's going on?" Nahlia asks, stepping out of her room.

"Go back and lay down," I say.

"But, what—" she begins.

"Nahlia, please go back into your room and lay down." She stops rubbing her eyes and closes the door.

I bolt down the stairs and kneel next to Pastor Clark. When I place my hand in front of his mouth, I can tell he is still breathing. I stand up and find the phone in the kitchen. I've never dialed 911, so I didn't know what to expect. The operator picks up and starts asking me basic questions. I answer and hang up the phone. I go back to Pastor Clark's side and begin to pray again. "You prepare a table before us in the presence of our enemies. You anoint our heads with oil; our cups overflow. Surely, goodness and mercy will follow us all the days of our life, and we will dwell in the house of the Lord forever. Amen."

CHAPTER 11: BRAYDEN FOSTER

Love Blind

∞ ∞ ∞

I awaken to darkness.

I try to move, but a sharp pain shoots through my tough yet fragile body. I whimper. The pain wipes out any excitement, any joy I have for life. Still, there is darkness. With every part of my body—including my eyelids—in agony, I can't decide which is worse, the pain or the dark. There is not even a trace of light to reveal where I am. I'm laying on something soft, but even a mountain of cotton balls would feel like a valley of thorns to my aching flesh.

Then the beeping starts. It's like thunder in the sky of my murky mind. *Beep! Beep! Beep! Beep!* I wrestle with the pain, as I attempt to lift my hands to my ears. *I hope I still have ears.*

"Brayden. Brayden," Jakes says. "Brayden! You're awake! I can't believe—"

"Shh…" I manage to say, after taking the deepest breath I can bear.

"Oh, I'm sorry," Jakes says. "I'm just happy, bro. You're awake. Everyone's been so worried about you."

"It hurts."

"What hurts?" Jakes asks.

"Everything," I say, groaning

"Well, do you want me to push the button on your bed for your pain meds? It's connected to your IV."

"Yes."

"Okay," he says. I assume he pressed the button because the beeping gets thrown off its rhythm. "There you go."

"Where am I?" I ask.

"You're in the hospital," Jakes says. "You were in the intensive care unit, but they switched you to a regular room."

"How long have I been here?"

"It's Monday morning. You've been here since Saturday. So, you've been here around 48 hours."

"What happened to my eyes?" I ask. "I can't see."

"You had some damage to your left eye, but they said they fixed you up," he says, sounding like he is standing right over me. "The doctor said you needed a few days to rest your eyes before you could take off the bandages. That should be now, so I'm sure you can take this mummy wrap off. In fact, let me buzz the nurse."

"Just take it off."

"Let me just buzz the—"

"Take it off," I say.

"Alright. Alright," Jakes says, moving closer. He places his hand behind my head and has me lift up a little. This would have been impossible a few moments ago, but the pain medication is starting to work. I still moan as he slides his firm hand down to the back of my neck. He slowly unravels the skintight gauze from around my head. When he finishes, Jakes places my head back on the thin hospital pillow and removes the two gauze squares that are resting on top of my eyes. "There you go. You should be able to see now."

Everything is white. I winch, as my eyes are violated by the overbearing light. "Cut the lights," I say. "It's too bright." I hear his twelve-inch feet trek to the far end of the room. Soon the brightness dims.

"Is that better?" Jakes asks.

"Much. Thank you." Jakes walks back to the edge of the bed. After my eyes finish adjusting, I take a look around. Balloons, half-eaten cake, and greasy pizza boxes litter the room.

"Where did all of this come from?" I ask, pointing to the wreckage.

"The team came through Saturday after practice," Jakes says.

"Where is everyone now?" I ask.

"Well…" He starts. "They…uh…were kind of—"

"Jakes," I say, "just tell me the truth. Why aren't any of them here?" Even in the dimmed lighting, I can see the discomfort creeping over his chiseled face. "Tell me." He starts pacing the floor at the end of the bed.

"They haven't been back since they found out," he says.

"Found out what?" I'm surprised I don't see blood streaming from his lips with how hard he is biting his tongue. "Come on, Jakes. I can handle it."

"They," he starts, "found out why you were attacked." I want to ask him how hard I can bite down without my tongue bleeding.

"Umm…okay," I say. "So, they left, and haven't been back?" He shakes his head like a shamed mother when their child has messed up at school. "How did they find out?"

"You had 'faggot' spray-painted on your back," Jakes says. "What happened that night, Brayden?"

"Where is my father?" I ask.

"Your father's secretary told me that he is out of town on a business trip overseas. He won't be back until next week. He called Coach though to check on you. Now, what happened Friday night?"

"Can you open the blinds a little?" I watch as Jakes walks over and pulls the cord to open the window so hard I think it might pop off. He walks back over to my side.

"What happened Friday?" he asks again, raising his voice. Apparently, this is the wrong time to practice biting my tongue. "Brayden, I promised that I would look out for you. I promised you that I would be there, and the same day I make the promise you end up in the hospital. Now, I feel bad enough as it is that I wasn't there for you. You have got to tell me what happened. I need to make this right." Despite the shadow the blinds have formed across his face, I can see Jakes' eyes beginning to get teary.

"I want to tell you," I say, "but I can't."

"Why not, Brayden?" he asks. "You have to tell me what happened to you?"

"I'm afraid of what you will do?"

"Just tell me!" Jakes screams.

"No."

"This is the worst thing you could do to me, man. I told you about what happened to my brother. You have to tell me." I stare at him like the veil is still covering my eyes. "Well, I can't do this right now. I'll be back later," Jakes says. "I'll send the doctor in on my way out." He snatches his coat off the counter and walks out the door.

I take the red button in my hand and press down in the vain attempt to release more pain meds. Soon, the nurse walks in.

"Hello, Mr. Foster," the nurse says. "Your brother told us you were awake. How are you feeling today?"

"It hurts," I say.

"What hurts?" she asks.

"Everything."

§§§§§

A few hours have passed, and Dr. Blount is sitting on the small rolling stool next to my bed.

"I hope you like the food here," Dr. Blount says, "because you're going to be here another week or so." Though his hair is entirely grey, he doesn't look much older than forty. The bulky, white lab coat he's wearing covers his slim frame. "Now, I have good news and bad news. Which, do you want first?"

"It doesn't matter," I say, watching him as he fidgets with his stethoscope.

"Okay," he says, sucking in air like a vacuum. "The good news is that you will recover fully; the bad news is that you will have to take it easy for another three months."

"What about basketball?" I ask, sounding wishful and hopeless at the same time.

"I'm sorry, Brayden," Dr. Blount says. "You're going to miss most of your practice season." I look out the open window. "You ought to feel lucky to be alive."

"Oh, yeah, I feel fortunate," I say.

"You'll cheer up soon, champ. In the meantime, you have plenty of morphine there to keep you as comfortable as possible. I can tell you have already become familiar with the red button." He laughs to himself but quickly stops when he realizes he is laughing alone. "I'll be checking on you." Dr. Blount taps the edge of the bed as he turns and disappears through the doorway.

Thirty minutes later, the door opens just as I begin to doze off. "Alright," the nurse says, "here's your room." She enters with two older male hospital employees. The guy with sandy blonde hair is pushing a stretcher with a relatively young black guy on there. "Try to move him gently to the bed guys, okay," she says. They hoist him off of the stretcher and put him in the bed in one swift motion.

"There you go," one of the men say.

"Thanks, guys," the nurse says, turning to the man lying in bed. As the two men exit, a glamorous, young woman enters. Maybe it's my eyes still adjusting, but her graceful stride looks like she's on a runway with the long silky strands of her black hair flowing in the stale hospital air.

"You look comfortable," the woman with black hair says.

"He certainly does," the nurse replies.

"I feel as comfortable as anyone can with a shaved head full of stitches," the guy says to them.

"Well," the black-haired woman says, "You are quite lucky that you didn't suffer a concussion or worse."

"We find people under the influence of alcohol are less prone to die from an accident and suffer fewer injuries," the nurse says.

"I don't even want to talk about alcohol right now," he says.

"Well, you need to talk about alcohol," the woman with black hair says, shaking a finger at him with the other hand clutching her hip.

"Okay," the nurse says, "I'll give you two some space and come by later to check on you." She walks over to me. "Are you okay?" she asks me.

"I'm pretty numb right now," I respond. "Have you heard anything from my father?"

"No. Not since you were checked in," the nurse says. I can tell she wants to change the subject. "I'll let you know as soon as he does, okay?"

"Yeah," I say, looking away.

"I'll be back to check on you a little later," she says. She scurries out of the room and, softly, shuts the door. I never knew, but it's harder to cry when you have two people beginning to raise their voices a few feet away from you. I can't say this is true in all instances, but definitely when you're in a hospital bed. My eyes close as I listen to the soap opera beside me.

"Call her again," I hear the man in the bed say.

"She doesn't want to talk to you," the black-haired woman says. "I told her you would be fine."

"Does she know I'm still here?" he asks.

"Yes. I told her they kept you over for observation," she says. "I don't care what you say right now; she's not coming."

"Where is my cell phone?" he asks.

"Right here," she says. I hear him pushing buttons on the phone. There is a moment of silence.

"Voicemail," he says.

"I told you," the woman with black hair says. "You proved her point last night. It seems you haven't learned anything from the book."

"I have changed," he says.

"Look at you? You're in the hospital. You haven't changed," she says. "Excuse me?" I feel a hand on my bed, causing me to look in that direction. "Excuse me? I'm sorry to bother you."

"It's cool," I say. "What's up?"

"What's up is I'm Gloria, and that is Oliver," she says, pointing to the man in the bed. "Who are you?"

"I'm Brayden."

"Brayden, what a beautiful name," she says. "Brayden?"

"Yes?" I reply.

"What happened to you?" she asks.

"Gloria…" Oliver says.

"What?"

"Leave the boy alone," he says.

"I'm not a boy," I say. "I can take care of myself."

"I'm sorry. I was just—" Oliver begins.

"It's cool. I just fell down some stairs," I say.

Gloria looks at me a moment. "Brayden," she says, "are you really going to try to tell me that—"

"Gloria…" Oliver says. "If the young man said he fell down stairs, he fell down stairs."

"Okay, okay," she responds, "stairs don't normally give you a black eye, but maybe the stairs you fell down know how to throw a punch."

"What do you want?" I ask, displaying the stark annoyance on my bruised face.

"Can you do me one favor?" Gloria asks.

"What's that?"

"Can you watch him, and make sure he doesn't drink anything other than water?" Gloria asks.

"Gloria," Oliver says.

"Sure," I say, looking over at him, "I can do that."

"Oh," Gloria says, leaning forward and whispering, "can you make sure he doesn't fall out of bed? I've seen the inside of enough hospitals to last me a lifetime."

"Okay," I say, struck by her approachable beauty. The girls I've met in California, like Brittany, are so pretentious that, despite their stunning looks, they're ugly. With a simple white T-shirt and slim-fit blue jeans, Gloria has a brilliance about her that seems nearly angelic.

"Great," she says in a soft, motherly tone. She doesn't look old enough to a mother, but she speaks like she has some experience. "Well, I'm going to leave you two to rest. Play nice." As she walks out, I turn back to the window.

§§§§§

Tuesday night comes, and Oliver and I have barely said enough to each other to form a complete thought. I'm lying in bed, flipping channels with the remote, when he wakes up from his nap. I can tell because the low growling from his throat stops. He stretches, looks up at the television mounted on the wall, and then looks at the clock across from it.

"Do you mind lowering the volume a bit?" he asks, flicking on the light over his head.

"Sure," I say, sliding my finger to the top of the remote to turn it off.

"You do not have to turn off the television for me," he says. "I am simply about to read, and want to be able to focus better."

"It's fine," I reply. "It's getting late anyway. I'm about to head to sleep."

"Okay," he says, grabbing the book that is on the small tray beside him.

I turn toward the window, placing my back at him. I've been trying to wean myself off of the medicine, using meditation techniques that Jakes taught me earlier. It was working more before, but for some reason, my pain is amplified at night. I'm pushing the red button when I hear a low moan. I turn over and ask, "Are you okay?"

"Why do you ask?" he inquires.

"I just heard you moaning."

"Oh, I was just reading to myself," he says.

"What book is that?"

"Well, the book is by a man named Ernest Lee, Minister Ernest Lee to be exact," Oliver says.

"What's it about?" I ask.

"The author expresses how the world has caused him great affliction because of the pieces in him that other people can't accept. The major premise of the book is love—or the lack thereof—in people's hearts."

"Wow," I say, "sounds like the world needs to read that one."

"Why do you say that?" he asks.

"Because, teammates, friends, even family will leave you if you tell them that you're somehow different than what they are used to. People don't even care how that makes you feel."

"Sounds like you know something about that first hand," he says, closing the book.

"I sure do."

"Does that have anything to do with your present situation?" he asks.

"Well, um…I guess you could say that."

"If you do not mind me asking, what really happened? We both know you did not fall down any stairs."

"I was beaten by some of my teammates," I said without looking at him.

"Was it over a girl?" he asks, raising an eyebrow.

"No," I say. "I guess you could say it happened because there was no girl."

"I am afraid I do not understand," he says. After a few moments of silence pass, he says, "I am sorry if my prying is causing you to feel uncomfortable. I can go back to reading this book and let you sleep."

"I'm here because I'm gay," I blurt out. "I should be able to tell a stranger if I can tell my father." I let silence fall like a lone feather from a bird in the sky. "I'm here because my teammates found out I liked guys and tried to kill me." I look back at the blank T.V. screen, waiting for him to find some words—any words—to say.

"I'm sorry to hear that," he finally says.

"Thank you," I reply.

"So are you ready to change?" he asks.

"Huh? What do you mean? Change what?"

"Well, after everything you went through, I am wondering if you are finally ready to change your ways," he says.

"What ways?"

"Look, I don't mean to be offensive," he says. "I'm a pastor." My heart nearly stops. "I'm now seeing that everything I went through was really to be in this hospital, just to help you come out of this lifestyle."

"Are you serious?" I ask.

"Yes. I am a pastor," he replies.

"No. When I just told you guys beat me because I was gay, did you ask me after that if I wanted to change?"

"Yes," he says, apparently not seeing anything wrong with his choice of words.

"So, I could have ended up paralyzed or with brain damage, and you wouldn't have cared?"

"I care, Brayden," he says, "but I care more about your soul than your physical body."

"No, you don't care about me," I say, attempting to sit up in my bed. "You can't care about my soul without caring about all of me. My soul is a part of me. That's like saying that you care for my bones but not my skin because it's going to decay. All you really see is a gay, black guy who has reaped the rewards of his lifestyle. You're supposed to be a pastor. You're supposed to love me no matter what."

"I do love you, but what you are doing is an aberration from the original design of mankind," he says. "So, I cannot apologize for asking that question."

"Who told you that?" I ask.

"God's Word tells me that."

"I heard your conversations with your wife on the phone today. Does God's Word tell you not to get drunk and fall down stairs? Is that your lifestyle?"

"You leave my wife out of this," he says.

"Why?" I ask. "You want me to show you compassion? You can't even ask if I'm okay after what I went through. You're so busy trying to judge me. Well, Jesus is my savior and not you. Jesus loves me. If I remember the stories correctly, it wasn't the regular people Jesus had the biggest problem with; it was the hypocritical priests. They didn't know how to show compassion. They didn't know how to love. So, you can sit there and judge me, but look in the mirror at the stitches in your own head."

"You don't think I see them?" he asks. "You don't think I know I have made mistakes?"

"You're not blind, but it's obvious that what you see has turned into a selfish lesson."

"What are you implying?" the pastor asks.

"I'm implying that you learned a lesson for you, but there is a greater lesson about how you treat other people now that you know what it's like to fall down. You fell because of what you did. I fell because of what was done to me. Losing blood wasn't my fault, but yours was. Yet, you sit in judgment of me? Jesus would be ashamed of your judgment because only the one without sin has a right to cast a stone."

"I'm not trying to throw stones at you," he says.

"That's what makes it so bad. You're not even trying, but you are." I turn over and face the window. "Keep reading your book, pastor. It seems like you have a lot more to learn." I pull the covers up around my neck. "Goodnight."

§§§§§

The Thursday morning light is crisscrossing my face, as the trees in front of the window sway in the autumn wind. I breathe in deep, wishing I could feel the fresh air against my nose hairs. No such luck. All I take in is the sour tension that is lingering between the pastor and me. Yesterday, we both made subconscious vows of silence towards one another. I didn't even glance at him. When Jakes came to visit, I had him pull the curtain that separates our beds. I didn't want to feel the pastor's cold eyes staring at us.

I roll onto my back and look up to see the same 52 ceiling tiles. From my peripheral vision, I notice the pastor's overhead light on.

"Good morning, Brayden," Oliver says.

"Good morning," I say, startled by his voice.

"Can we converse for a moment?"

"Sure. Not like I have anywhere to go," I say, facing him. I notice that he has the same book in his lap.

"I want to start by saying I apologize for my words the other day." He sits up in his bed, rearranging the white sheets covering his legs. "I believe what I said was right, but it wasn't at the right time. I was insensitive during a time when you need support. Please accept my apologies for that."

"I can respect that," I say, smiling on the inside. "I forgive you."

"I have never actually met anyone who was gay," he says.

"Yes, you have," I reply. "How old are you?"

"I will be celebrating my 30th birthday in just a few months," Oliver says.

"So, you're almost 30 and work in the church. Whether you knew it or not, you have met gay people."

He laughs, somewhat uncomfortably. A wistful smile appears as he pauses to think.

"Brayden, do you mind me asking a question?"

"Go right ahead," I reply.

"When did you start feeling gay?"

"Probably around the time you started feeling straight," I say, trying not to laugh.

"I'm serious. I am trying to understand your point of view. I must admit that I have never sat down and spoken to someone who identified as being gay. I know what I know to be true, and that is it."

"That's the funny thing about truth, we make it our reality, and not much matters after that," I say.

"You are not going to sway my belief, but I do want to understand at least," he says, placing his hands in his lap.

"Well, when did you feel straight?" I ask.

"I don't know if I would say I felt straight. I just am."

"Great place to start. I just am," I say.

"Were you molested as a child or had sex early?" he asks.

"No, but even if I were, I don't believe it would change who I am attracted to."

"Well then, what makes someone take up the gay lifestyle?" he asks.

I breathe in deep. "What makes you take up the straight lifestyle? This isn't a choice," I say.

"Yes, it is. You choose who you will sleep with," he replies.

"I agree," I say. "You can choose who you sleep with, just as you can choose who you don't sleep with, but that doesn't change what you like. A nun or priest can take vows of celibacy, but that won't change who they are attracted to. In fact, I have never had real sex, but I know I like men. I grew up with a father. I've played sports all of my life. I've dated girls. I've done everything a normal guy would do, but I still like men."

"So you don't think it's a lifestyle at all?" he asks.

"What I know is that being gay is as much a part of me as my skin color or hair color. I can bleach my skin and dye my hair, but that only changes how it looks, not what it is. It will always go back to being what it was intended to be."

"The other day, you were quoting scriptures. I take it you know what the Bible says about homosexuality," he says.

"I know what the Bible says," I respond. "I come from a model Christian home—Sunday School and all."

"So, how do you feel about going against that?" He asks.

"I feel the same way you must feel," I say.

"What do you mean?"

"Well," I say, "blacks aren't slaves anymore."

"Correct," he says.

"Did that happen because of the work of abolitionists and civil war?" I ask.

"Indeed."

"Two scriptures come to mind: Thou shall not kill, and slaves obey your masters."

"I see where you're going," he says.

"I'm just saying, Pastor. You aren't a slave today because the people during that time went against two scriptures in the Bible, one of which is a part of the Ten Commandments." He is fidgeting in his bed. "How do you justify that? Would you say the abolitionists were wrong for their pursuit of equality for all people?"

"Don't try to sway what I believe," he snaps. "I believe the Bible is infallible."

"That's fine, Pastor. I would hope you believe what you preach. I'm not trying to convert you to believe one thing over another. That's the difference between you and me. I can accept you as an alcoholic pastor, but you can't accept I'm gay. Now, remember, you asked me these questions. I'm just answering."

"I do accept you," he says. "I just can't accept your sin."

"What if I believe what you call sin is a natural part of me? Can you still accept me?" He becomes still, staring at the white sheets that cover him to his bruised hips. After a minute, he faces me.

"I just heard what you said. Knowing what you know about me being a pastor and what I've done, you still accept me?" he asks.

"Yes," I say. "I may not think your actions deserve my acceptance, but your humanity demands it."

"No one but my wife would say something so filled with sincerity and love," he says, looking back at the sheets.

"Wow. Then, it is a shame that the Bible says that she and every other woman are supposed to keep quiet in church. I'm sure you follow that scripture too."

"If I did, I would be in this hospital bed for a completely different reason altogether." Smiles envelop our tense faces, as our laughter freshens the sterile air in the room. He takes the book out of his lap. "I want you to have this," he says, tossing the book into my lap.

Someone gave it to me who wanted me to learn how to love. Consider this my gift to you for helping me learn a valuable lesson in love."

"Thank you," I say, stunned by his change of heart.

"I do love you, Brayden. I love you as Christ would love you, not for what you have done, are doing, or will do. I love you unconditionally, as you have shown me, unconditional love. I thought I was here to help you, but it seems I'm in this bed so I can learn from you. I don't agree with you, but that doesn't have to make me disagreeable. I once was blind, but now I see."

"I didn't expect you to say that at all. So, I guess we are both learning from each other," I say. I begin flipping through the book, but my mind is really on my father. I close my eyes and silently pray that God would use this same love to cure my father's blindness.

§§§§§

Chapter 12: Oliver Clark, Jr.

Measured Truth

∞ ∞ ∞

"Hey, hey," Gloria says, walking into the hospital room with Nahlia, "Are you ready to eat something?"

"Good afternoon," I reply. "I was just listening to my stomach growl like a dog when you try to take its bone."

"Well, let's put that dog to rest," Gloria replies.

"Mom," Nahlia says, "when are we going to get a dog?"

"Honey, can we talk about this after I find a job?" Gloria asks. Nahlia nods her head and walks towards the doorway. Gloria moves closer towards me and leans in. "Are you really ready to do this?"

"I have to, Gloria," I say, whispering back. "It's the right thing to do."

"I know that, Oliver. I'm asking if you are ready to do it?"

"Ready or not, I must," I say, turning my head from Gloria, as Nahlia walks back towards us.

"Excuse me," Nahlia says. Our stares signal to her to commence talking. "Aren't ya'll hungry?"

"You sound like Oli," I say. "You two could be brother and—"

"Let's get you out of bed, and save the biology lesson for dinner," Gloria says, gripping my knee.

"I think the pills they have prescribed for me are causing me to have loose lips," I say, sitting up in the bed.

"You might need to check and make sure you haven't had these pills before, because your lips have been pretty loose since I've known you." While we are laughing, she glances at Brayden. "I see you gave him the book."

"Yes," I say, "I did. It seemed like the right thing to do after you inadvertently passed it my way."

"I'm sure Ernest Lee would be happy to know his book was helping connect people," Gloria says. "I just wish Brayden was up so I could talk to him about it."

"Mom," Nahlia says, gripping her sides, "I'm ungry!"

"Nahlia, calm down," Gloria says, pointing her finger back without looking in her direction.

"Gloria," I say, gripping my side, "I'm ungry too." The room fills with so much laughter, I think that we might wake up Brayden, but he doesn't budge.

"Now it is official," Gloria says.

"What's that?" I ask.

"Those meds are doing more than giving you loose lips."

§§§§§

The elevator dings, indicating we have reached the first floor of the hospital. "I hope the food is better down here than what they give me in my room," I say.

"You certainly deserve it," Gloria says.

"Why do you say that?" I ask.

"Well, this is your first time in almost a week that you have spared everyone from looking at you in a gown. So, I would say you deserve a pretty good meal for that."

I stop walking down the corridor and look at Gloria. "Why does everyone around me think they are comedians?"

"I think you're so not funny that everyone else's funniness levels go up around you," she says, continuing to walk down the hall. "You hit your head, sir. You didn't break your legs, so come on." Hearing her talk to me like that only makes me think of Rachel and how much I miss her." I resume walking but now with a heavy heart. Gloria looks over her shoulder and sees my turbid countenance. She walks back to my side and asks, "What's wrong?"

"I miss her," I say.

"I know you do. But, you have to focus on this. This is your priority right now. We can talk about your wife after this. You have a little girl who needs you focused on her."

"Gloria," I say, "you are absolutely right. Thank you."

"You're welcome," she responds. "Oh, Oliver."

"Yes?"

"Are you still ungry?" she asks, clutching her sides.

As we make our way through the broad blue metal doors, our laughter fills the cafeteria. I tend to keep public opinions and impressions as a top priority, but my hysterical laughter doesn't concern me at all. "I'm a little bit lighter," I say.

"Huh?" she asks.

"I feel lighter. For once, I feel a sense of truth coming to my life that I haven't felt before. I have been hiding in the shadows of secrets and heavy expectations all of my life. Today, I am free to laugh and enjoy life a little bit lighter. I think I got so good at wearing masks that I forgot how remarkable it feels to live in truth. Truth does make us free. I haven't even told Nahlia yet, but I feel freer now with just the will to tell her."

"Amazing what a little truth can do, huh?" she asks, tapping my chest as she grabs a tray.

"Yeah. Being a pastor, you would think I would be the master of truth, right?"

"Don't beat yourself up," she says. "All of us want to cover ourselves.

We just have to remember that the best cover is the truth and not deception."

"Preach, sister!" I shout. "That makes me feel like tossing this tray down and running around this cafeteria."

"You aren't going to start convulsing like the people at your church, are you?"

"Gloria, it's called 'shouting,'" I say.

"Shouting, hopping, convulsing, it's the same thing. You just better be careful of all of that in here."

"Why is that?" I ask.

"This is a hospital. Do I really need to say more than that?" Nahlia walks up and interrupts our laughter.

"Mom, you're embarrassing me," Nahlia says, tugging on her mother's elbow.

"Okay, okay," Gloria says. "We will behave. Why don't you go get what you want and go to the register?"

"Alright," Nahlia says, walking towards the pizza.

"I can't help but acknowledge how much she reminds me of Oli," I say, following Nahlia.

"They are family," she says.

"I know, but I never thought my family would be in this situation."

"I never thought I would be in some of the situations I'm in now either, but I live with it," she snaps.

"Whoa!" I say, "I come in peace. I did not mean to offend you."

"I'm sorry," Gloria says. "You didn't. I walk around with a few secrets myself."

"Gloria, I'm here for you."

"I know you are," she says.

"I don't say that because I'm a pastor. I'm saying that because you are my family, and I consider you a friend."

"Thank you, Oliver," she replies, tossing down her tray and maneuvering under my arms to hug me. "You don't know how much I needed to hear that. It's been so long since I had a friend."

"Well, you have one now," I say, placing my tray next to hers. I squeeze Gloria tight, feeling like she is loving new life into me. In the same day, a gay guy and a former stripper were able to love my bitter, wife-abusing, alcoholic nature. What's sad is that before meeting them, I would not have been unable to accept and love them. "I love you," I say, as my mind lingers on the scripture: "God is love."

I weep. The dampness forming on my shoulder lets me know that I'm not alone in shedding tears. Gloria's embrace becomes more of a bearhug, as I feel her trying to regain her composure. Although gathering emotions is as arduous as carrying water in hand, we release our embrace, select and pay for our food, and find seats in an area void of people.

"Nahlia," Gloria says, "we need to have a big girl talk with you today, okay?"

"Alright," she says, shrugging her shoulders and leaning her head to the side. Gloria looks at me and nods.

"Nahlia," I say, "umm, well…it appears that I…umm…you…we are…what I am trying to say is that—"

"Look here my little angel," Gloria says. "Remember when I told you that your father died a long time ago?"

"Yeah," Nahlia says.

"Well, that wasn't entirely true," Gloria says, reaching for her daughter's hand. "He did die, but he only died a little over a month ago."

"How do you know?" Nahlia asks.

"I know," I say, "because he was my father as well." Nahlia's face scrunches up in confusion. "I am your brother." Nahlia enters a trance of shock that is only solved by getting approval from her mother. Gloria nods at her.

"Are you okay, Nahlia?" her mother asks.

"Yeah," she replies.

"Okay. I think I better leave you two alone for a minute," Gloria says, standing up from the table. "Just let me know when you're ready."

She grabs her tray of Chinese food and walks to another table a few feet away.

Nahlia continues to stare at me. "What are you thinking, dear?" I ask.

"She's going to be okay," she says. A mature tear rolls down her adolescent face.

"Who is going to be okay?" I ask.

"I prayed that God would send my mom an angel to watch over her because I was scared for her."

"I know there have been some scary moments for you," I say, handing her a napkin to wipe her tears. She nods her head in agreement.

"I was really scared that God didn't care about us anymore," she says, looking away from me.

"Why did you bring your mother to the church if you didn't believe God cared?" I ask, curious about her thought process.

"I remembered that on one of your shows you said that God loves everyone," she says. "That made me think that God still loves my mom too."

"God does love everyone," I say. "Is that what made you pray for an angel?"

"Yeah. I knew I couldn't be with my mom all the time, so she needed someone to protect her."

"Well, that's a great thing to pray for," I say. "You are more selfless than many of the older people at my church. So, do you believe your angel is helping your mom?"

"Yes!" Nahlia's eyes twinkle from the mixture of tears and blissful optimism.

"Why do you believe that?"

"You know."

"What do you mean?"

"You know why I believe that," she says.

"Nahlia, I really don't know what you are talking about."

"You're our angel," she says, looking at me like a child stares at a department store Santa hoping they are the real thing.

"Me?"

"Yes."

"I'm no angel," I say.

"Yes, you are. You've helped us out so much.

"I just don't think I'm an—" I begin.

"Can you tell me about our dad?" All of the salivae in my mouth turns into cement.

"He was an interesting guy," I say, feeling like my heart is an animal trying to break out of its cage.

"Okay. Why was he interesting?" Nahlia asks.

"He just was," I reply.

"You didn't like him very much did you?"

"Why would you say something like that?" I ask.

"Normally, people have good things to say about the people they love. It should be easy right?" I fidget in my chair and look up at the ceiling like I'm in the waiting room after being called to the principal's office. When my eyes pan back to Nahlia's cheerful countenance, I say the only thing that makes sense to my heart.

§§§§§

When I step in front of my hospital room door, I'm confident I made the right choice of what to share with Nahlia. Stepping inside, I find my assistant—Shaw—, Terry and Jakes sitting around Brayden's bed. "Good day," I say. "What's going on in here?"

"Hey," Brayden says, "we were just talking about football."

"How are you, Pastor?" Shaw asks.

"I'm just fine. Thank you." I reply.

Terry stands up and walks up to me. "You need some help, old man?" he asks, barely able to contain his laughter.

"Go sit down, Terry," I say, swatting his hands away from my arms. "What are you doing here, anyway? Don't the deacons have a board meeting tonight?"

"It was canceled," Terry replies.

"Canceled?" I ask. "Who canceled it?"

"Deacon DuBois canceled it. He said there was something more pressing that he needed to prepare his case for during our next meeting."

"Did he suggest the nature of this pressing item?"

"Not at all, but I found out that he plans on organizing a quick vote to remove you from office at the end of the month," Terry says.

"I can handle that when I get out of here," I say, sitting on the edge of the bed.

"Yes, we can," Terry says. "But, you don't seem surprised at all."

"This is just church politics. I expected it sooner."

"Okay. In other news, it's good to see you up in some real clothes and not those gowns."

"Well, you are about to see me back in that hospital gown, because I'm getting back in bed," I say.

"It's not so bad," Brayden says.

"What's that?" asks Terry.

"The gown."

"It's bad if you're not at practice," Jakes says, bumping the bed with his knee.

"I guess I can't argue with that," Brayden responds. "Oh, I just wanted to make sure I thanked you for this book." Brayden reaches out his arm and taps the book on the table next to him. "It's perfect."

"I figured you would like it," I say.

"What book is that?" Terry asks. "I don't know about any book."

"You don't like to read, Terry," I say. "Why would I give you a book?"

"I was a Pre-Law major, Junior. What would make you think I can't read?" Terry asks.

"I didn't say you could not read," I say. "I said you do not like to read. You had to read for college, but you didn't like it."

"I guess I can't argue with that," Terry says, looking at Brayden and grinning.

"Well, I'm curious too. What's the book about?" Jakes asks.

Brayden grabs the book from the table, and says, "It's about love. In fact, it's about the absence of love."

"Okay. You have my attention. Go on," Terry says.

Brayden opens the book up and flips through some pages. "I think this is a good place to start," he says, beginning to read from the book:

> Now, I'm on a mission for love. As the Statue of Liberty is a symbol of hope and indiscriminate love, I desire to display a love that shines so bright the lost are found. I want my life's love to shine like a torch in the wilderness, guiding the tired, poor, and huddled masses into a promised land of love without end. Those who yearn

to break away from the refuse of Hatred's shore and breathe the air of freedom, they will find the nation of my heart pure and open to embracing their tempest-tossed souls. I want to love the abused and scorned, lame and untamed. I want to love the homo, the hopeless, the hurt, and the heartless. The gangster, the thief, the killer, and the chief all are worthy of this love I want to share. I want to love what others throw away: the woman, the man, the in-between, the rich, the rapper, the slut, the saint, the bitter, the broken, and diseased. God, help me to love what others throw away, even me. Help me to love all of me.

After we discuss the book for a few hours, the guys begin to depart. Jakes is shaking my hand, but I notice that Shaw is writing something down on one of the hospital napkins. As Terry comes over to my side to hug me, I lose my visual of Shaw.

When Terry lets go, I watch as Shaw walks away from Brayden's bedside. Brayden flashes a smile at me as Shaw heads over to hug me and exits. Brayden and I are left in the room.

I look over to Brayden and ask, "Did he give you his number?"

"Who?" he asks.

"I am asking if Shaw gave you his number."

"He did."

"Why did he do that?" I ask.

He adjusts his pillow, saying, "You should ask him yourself."

"Okay. Goodnight, Brayden. Rest well."

"You do the same, Pastor," he says.

"You know…I really do want to love on the level that Ernest Lee speaks about," I say.

"I do too. I believe if you want to, you can. We have to be honest about how we have loved up until now, which isn't easy to accept and express. Let's agree to accept how we have loved in the past and what we can do to love better in the future."

I pause and take a deep breath, "Let us do just that."

Chapter 13: Gloria Sanchez

The World is Round

∞ ∞ ∞

The pastor is home, and I feel like such a failure.

I place my loaned key into the keyhole that isn't attached to anything I own. Here I am, a damn good mother, a strong Latino woman, and I can't do anything for my daughter, for myself. It's been difficult being here with the Clarks. While it's far from perfect, they have their own lives: income, house, cars, everything. I have my daughter sleeping in a stranger's house. I thought I was better than this.

I open the front door, walk in and shut the front door behind me, hoping not to be seen or heard. As soon as I place my foot on the bottom step, it squeaks. Pastor calls my name through his study door, "Gloria. Gloria." I set my foot on the second step, but the first step begins to squeal as I release my other foot off it. Soon, Pastor's study door is open, and his head is poking out.

"Gloria, what are you doing?" he asks.

"Oh, I was just about to take a quick nap," I say, placing my right foot on the third step.

"Before you do that, would you please converse with me for a few moments?"

"Oh, okay." He holds the door open for me as I come near him. When I pass through the doorway, he holds out his arms and pulls me into a hug.

"Gloria, I want to thank you for being a friend. We may not have known each other long, but you have already proven to be a loyal and trustworthy person. For that I want to thank you," he says, releasing from one of the only warm embraces I've had in years. My body continues to tingle with a breathtaking sensation as he walks towards his desk. Maybe this is what the girls at the club felt like when they were on drugs. It feels like he just injected me with more love and hope than I've felt, outside of my daughter.

"One of the primary reasons why pastors go crazy is because we have few people in our lives that we can share our hearts with who will not respond in judgment. No one but another pastor can know the immense pressure of perfection that pastors encounter. We can laugh but not too hard. We can cry but not too long. We can barely get upset, rarely disagree, and never make a mistake or misstep."

"Those expectations seem unrealistic," I say, watching him sit in his chair, as my body simmers down.

"That is because they are," Pastor Clark says. "Please, don't get me wrong. I believe that clergy ought to be held to a higher standard. The bar should be higher, but no one—not even a person of the cloth—can be perfect."

"How do you deal with that?" I ask.

"You have seen how many of us deal with it. Just look at me. No, not every pastor drinks or does what my father did, but most of us struggle with some heavy burden in secret."

"Can't you just talk to another pastor?" I ask.

"I could, but they gossip too. Finding friends amongst pastors is difficult because there is often a measure of competition. There shouldn't be, but there is. Nevertheless, this is not why I called you here. I want to know why you have been avoiding me."

"I wouldn't say I've been avoiding you," I say. "I've just been busy looking for jobs."

"Gloria, I would like to think that I'm pretty good at reading people. I can feel that you have shifted somehow in your interaction with me. What happened?" My hands tighten. "I did what you wanted me to do. I told Nahlia how great her father was, and how he would have been there if he knew about her," he says. To save myself from crying, I lower my head and squish my lips together like I'm about to kiss a frog. "You have helped me with my secrets," he says. "Now, let me help you with yours—as a friend."

I look up at him and say, "I didn't want you to come home yesterday."

"Gloria, what exactly do you mean?" he asks.

"I mean that I didn't want you to come home yesterday," I repeat.

"I was only in the hospital for five days. Did you want me to be home sooner than that?"

"No," I say, shaking my head.

"Well, are you saying you wanted me there longer?"

"Yes," I say.

"Why would you wish something like that on me?" he asks, raising his eyebrow.

"With you back home, I'm reminded of how unnecessary I am to this house. In all the commotion with you, my life was given some purpose. I had an assignment. Now, my life is back to having no purpose. I don't have a job or have my own place to stay. I can't even buy my own food," I say, trying to remind myself why I just thought I was strong. "I just spent another day trying to find any decent work, only to be laughed at because I have no real work experience. I even tried to get another stripping job."

"Gloria—"

"Don't worry. Stain made sure that no club in a hundred-mile radius will hire me. On top of that, I found out I have..." I look away.

"Have what?" he asks, handing me some tissue. By now, my nose is running like a track star. I blow my nose and stare at the tissue as I fold it into a square. "Keep going. Don't stop sharing your truth with me now."

"I found out I have HIV, and I...I don't know what to do." My hands grip my head as it falls towards my lap. "My whole world is falling apart. I can't take anymore." For a moment, I feel like I might drown in this puddle of sorrow in my lap.

"Can I share something with you?" he asks, already moving to the chair beside me.

"Yeah," I say between sobs.

"Your world isn't flat," he says, placing his hand on my back.

"What does that mean?" I ask, lifting my head up.

"Many centuries ago, people believed that the world was flat. In their minds, you could actually sail to the edge of the Earth and fall off. Can you imagine living during an era like that?"

"No."

"But, you do," he says. "If you don't believe me, think of how many times you allow challenges to prevent you from going beyond where you are and what you know. Science proved that the world was round. You need to let your faith debunk the myth that your world is flat."

"I don't feel like I have any faith left," I say, looking at the picture on the wall of a man surrounded by lions.

Pastor Clark turns his head and looks at the picture. "That is Daniel from the Bible," he says, pointing at the black man in a loincloth. He was thrown into a lion's den simply for doing what he knew was right. He did not deserve it, but it happened. Maybe he thought it was more than he could handle, just like you do now, but by morning, not only was he alive, there was not even a scratch on his body."

"Well, I got more than scratched," I say.

"I know you did, but you weren't consumed. In some form, I believe Daniel heard God tell him what I am telling you now: Your world is round, not flat. So, even when you feel like you have reached your end and feel like you've taken all you can, you must keep going, and you will discover there is still more left in you. You are protected so you can fulfill your purpose."

"But, God doesn't speak to me."

"Gloria," he says, "whenever something is created that is God speaking. Nine years ago, when Nahlia was born, God spoke. When you were planted in your mother's womb, God spoke. At some point, God spoke and made sure our lives would cross paths. So, from my perspective, you're wrong. God has spoken to you more than you know; you just have to be listening."

"I guess you're right," I say, standing up. "Thank you, Oliver."

"You're welcome, Gloria," he replies, standing beside me.

"I have to stop now. I've been crying too much recently," I say.

"Well, let me say one last thing before you go. I know you think you are having difficulty hearing God, but I think I heard God pretty clear this week. I see a greater purpose in why I am led to ask you this question."

"What question?" I ask.

"How would you like to be my new administrative assistant?"

My eyes nearly pop out of their sockets. "Me?" I'm placing one hand on my chest and the other to my leaky eyes.

"Yes, you. You would have full health benefits. You don't have to answer now. I just wanted to—"

"Oh, thank you," I say, locking my arms around his waist and digging my head into his chest. "Thank you," I say, squeezing tighter.

"It's the least I can do," Pastor Clark says.

"You're an angel in disguise," I say, without letting go.

"Thank you, Gloria," he says. "It seems I was an angel unaware."

§§§§§

After picking up Nahlia from school, I came home and took a peaceful nap. I look at the clock: 6 p.m. Rolling out of bed like a stiff corpse, I forget I still have my clothes on from earlier. I yawn, stretching my arms over my head before making my way downstairs. Turning the corner from the wide staircase, I head towards the kitchen to grab something to drink. I can hear Oliver talking to another guy, as I walk past the office.

"It matters to me," Oliver says.

"Why?" the other man asks.

"I'm the pastor, and I have enough trouble on my hands already without the people working for me getting caught up in scandals."

"So, this is all about you?" the other man asks.

"No. That is not what I am trying to imply," Oliver says.

"What are you implying then?" the other man asks.

"I love you like a son, but I just can't—" Oliver begins.

"I'm sorry, pastor. Either you love me like a son or say what you are about to say. I won't listen to you try to fit in both with a 'but' in between. I've cleaned up your messes and covered you more times than I can remember. How can you suspend me from serving in the church when this is the only thing I've ever done that you don't agree with?"

"I am protecting you," Oliver says.

"No, you're protecting yourself. What I want to know is whether or not you are going to suspend yourself from preaching for what you did?"

"You know I can't do that," Oliver responds.

"But, you can punish me in a way that you wouldn't punish yourself? I respect you as my pastor. I even love you as a father figure, but I am certain about who I am. I love who I love. If you can't accept that, if you believe the Bible says you can't have me in your church because of what I feel inside of me, then I don't need to be at your church."

"Then get out!" Oliver shouts.

"You can push me away, but do you even know what are you pushing me to? You don't even care! The only scandal here is how hypocritical you are."

"Shaw, wait!" Oliver says as the study door swings open. I step back, as the young guy from church with the stylish, multi-colored glasses brushes past me. He heads right out of the front door, slamming it so hard I thought the hinges would crack. "Well, Gloria, you might as well come in."

"What was that about?" I ask, stepping into the room.

"I think—" he begins.

Ding dong!

"Ugh," I say. "Did I ever tell you that your doorbell is loud enough to wake Sleeping Beauty?"

"Sleeping Beauty?" he asks.

"Sorry for the children's book reference, but I haven't read anything but Ernest Lee's book and Nahlia's. I'll go get the door for—"

"Hey," a deep voice says from behind, startling me.

"Terry," Oliver says, standing up.

"Junior," Terry says, "sorry to interrupt. The door was unlocked." I side-step as the tall, black man steps toward Oliver's desk.

"Then why would you ring the doorbell?" Oliver asks.

"I was just letting you know I was coming in," Terry replies, as he holds out his chiseled arms. "Is everything alright? I saw Shaw running out of here, looking—"

"Everything will be just fine, Terry," Pastor says, embracing him. "I was just conversing with Gloria." I usually have plenty to say. But I couldn't form a three-letter word in Scrabble when Terry comes over.

"Gloria, it's good to see you again," Terry says, extending his bulky hand.

"Good to see you too," I say, avoiding eye contact as I turn to walk out of the room.

"Where are you going?" Terry asks.

"I'm leaving you two to talk."

"Oh, no. Stay. Sit," Terry replies.

"That sounds a lot like dog commands to me," I say, shaking my head and waving my index finger like I'm directing the church choir.

"I…I—" Terry begins.

"Gloria," Oliver says, "I can assure you Terry meant no harm. Please join us."

"Okay, but if Terry tells me to roll over, I'm out of here," I say, causing the room to fill with laughter.

Terry is now staring at me. Oliver is too busy laughing to notice, but, once he does, he asks Terry, "What is that in your hand?"

"It's a letter for you," he says, breaking his gaze.

"Who is it from?" Oliver asks.

"Your father," he says.

"He's dead."

"Yes, he is," Terry says, "but he left this for you. He told me to give it to you when you were ready." He hands Oliver the envelope, which he reluctantly takes from Terry. "I wanted to give it to you every time I came up to the hospital, but it just didn't feel right." Oliver down stares at the envelope for a moment.

"I can't," he says.

"You can't what?" I ask.

"I can't open it." Oliver looks up at me. "Will you read this to me?" he asks.

"Do you really want her reading this?" Terry asks. "You don't know what it says. What if—"

"I trust her, Terry," Oliver says, waving his hand like he's silencing an orchestra. "Will do you read it for me?" he asks me again.

"Sure," I say, reaching my right hand towards him. He passes the postcard-shaped envelope to me.

"Wait..." he says, turning to his desk, "use this to open it." Oliver reaches down in a drawer and grabs a silver letter opener. "My father gave it to me, so I guess it would be appropriate to use it now." Oliver passes me the letter opener. I stick it in the open space of the envelope, pulling up until the paper cleanly rips open. After handing him back the sharp, metal letter opener, I unfolder the letter with both hands. I glance up at Oliver. After an abrupt nod, I begin to read.

"To my only son," I say, clearing my throat:

> I will make this brief because I know how you feel about me. You are my son, and I am your father. I have watched you grow into an honorable man and a faithful pastor. While my achievements will beget lasting public celebration, I know the most prominent recollections you will bear highlight my multifarious mistakes. Unfortunately, I realized the ferocity of my actions when I was too old and obstinate to amend my recklessness. In a moment of clarity, I must impart in you the best that I possess—wisdom learned from my indiscretions. What I am about to disclose is by no means easy for me to share, but I feel indebted to you and the success of your leadership. Pastoring was rewarding yet wearisome. It wasn't the preaching or the politics that exhausted by zeal; it was the endless hiding. Mahatma Gandhi once wrote, 'Freedom is not worth having if it does not include the freedom to make mistakes.'

"Can you read that line again for me, Gloria," Oliver says.

"'Freedom is not worth having if it does not include the freedom to make mistakes,'" I read.

"Wow. Okay," he says. "Keep going."

Unfortunately, my renown and success in the community negated the luxury of such freedom. I've spent countless years warding off depression like a lone soldier with a stick against an army of guns. I preached love and forgiveness, but who was there to forgive me? For a pastor, when people say they pardon you, there within them a nagging essence of umbrage that lingers in their hearts. I impart this to you knowing that you now take my post. Don't allow your successes hail you while your secrets haunt you. Don't be afraid to open up and talk to Terry; he is a true friend and brother.

I look up as Terry and Oliver flash glances at each other and smile. I continue reading:

Now, I must divulge my gravest error. Your mother was light amid my darkness. I loved her. God rest her soul. But my violations were not inflicted upon you alone. I was unfaithful to her more than once. I visited exclusive and confidential clubs with young strippers. I am exposing this, knowing you have secrets. Enable my next words to protect you as you have safeguarded my legacy all these years. I was rarely unaccompanied during my escapades; Deacon DuBois was a frequent companion. While he remains my closest friend, he will remain your most significant opposition. He knows the Bible, but he has a corrupted heart. I am not ignorant of the reality to the selfish motive of his covering my actions because of our mutual sin. His narcissism will not lend you the same grace. So below, I have attached the places, dates, and times that we frequented those dens of iniquity. Use wisely. I trust your judgment both as a man and pastor. Know I love you, and I am sorry. Not perfect but seeking perfection, Dad, the Senior.

I look up and see tears flowing effortlessly down Oliver's cheeks.

"Junior, your old man loved you," Terry says, seizing and shaking Oliver's shoulder.

"It looks like he did," I agree.

"What in the hell is this?" Oliver asks, swatting Terry's hand away. "This can't be real."

"I know it's a lot to process," Terry says. "You just need to see how—"

"I needed to see him love me just one day while he was alive," Oliver says.

"You did," Terry says. "He was alive when he wrote this, and now you see it. Be glad you can let him rest in peace, knowing that he actually loved you more than you know or believe."

"I guess you are right," Oliver says. "If you two don't mind, I need some time alone."

"Sure, Junior," Terry says. "Just know I'm here when your thick head is ready to talk." He hugs Oliver and steps back to wait for me.

"I'm right upstairs if you need me, Oliver," I say. "You should know where to find that." Terry smiles.

"I think I do," Oliver says. "Thank you both. I love you."

Both Terry and I respond in harmony, "I love you too." I give Oliver a hug and walk out of the study. Terry holds the door open for me, closing it when he steps out behind me. As I head toward the kitchen, Terry calls my name.

"Yes?" I reply, turning to look at him.

"Umm…I thought you were going up to your room."

"Are you about to give me another dog order?"

"Oh, no. I wouldn't do—"

"I'm just messing with you," I say, resuming my walk towards the kitchen.

"So…," he says, causing me to twirl back around like a lazy ballerina. He has something familiar in his eye that reminds me of every man that tried to have me at the club. It's a look of longing. "I was thinking that maybe you and I could grab a bite to eat someday."

"Yes, Terry, that would be just fine," I say, ushering him to the front door.

"Great!" he exclaims. "How about we go out tomorrow night?"

"Actually," I say, opening the door, "I have an even better idea."

"What's that?" I make sure he is through the doorway before I answer.

"I'll see you on Sunday," I say with a smile.

"But, we have Sunday dinner here at the house," he replies.

"Exactly. Let's leave it at that. Goodbye."

I leave that tall mountain of a man staring at the front side of the door. I peek out the window and watch as he steps back and turns toward his car. I smile. It's funny how, in one moment, a man can make you feel that you're not so unlovable after all.

§§§§§

CHAPTER 14: BRAYDEN FOSTER

To Protect and Serve

 ∞ ∞ ∞

"Did you call him?"

"Yes, Shaw," I say, sitting on the edge of my hospital bed.

"Well, where is he?" he asks. With all his pacing, I'm surprised there aren't footprints in the tile.

"Shaw," I say, "calm down, sit back, and be patient. He'll be here in a minute."

Shaw freezes and steps back, sitting in the chair behind him. "I'm just saying that I can just as easily take you home in my car, Brayden."

"I know," I reply. "But, he needs to take me back to campus."

Shaw folds his arms. "You still haven't told me why."

"I know I haven't," I say. "Just know it's complicated."

"Okay," he says, "I'll leave it alone. I'm glad that you have people that care about you. I just wanted to show you that I care too."

"I can tell you care, and I appreciate it. Just don't give me any drama today, okay? I have a feeling there is going to be enough of that to last a lifetime."

"So, I shouldn't bring you any drama today. Check! What about tomorrow? Can I bring you drama then?"

We laugh a bit. As I look down, I see my untied shoe lashes. "Only if you plan on making that the last day you bring me anything. Ow!"

"What's wrong?"

"I'm still sore," I say. "I don't know why I thought I could put my foot on the bed to tie this shoe. Let me do it for you," Shaw says, hopping up and dashing over to my side.

"I'm not going to argue with you," I say. "I've been meaning to ask you something."

"What's that?"

"Are you going to speak with Pastor Clark again?"

"No, and I never will!" Shaw's thundering voice startles me momentarily.

"Hey, hey, hey!" I say, as he forcefully tightens my shoelace. "Don't take it out on the ankle."

"I'm sorry," he says, looking up at me. "I just can't believe what he said to me. Ugh!"

"Did you read that book I gave you?"

"Most of it," he says.

"Well, what you read should be enough to help you realize that a response of anger and hate will only create more hostility. There is no love in hate and no hate in love. Even when we are faced with hatred, we must think of Ernest Lee's words: 'We must envision smiles on unfriendly faces and extended hands on clenched fists.'"

Shaw looks at me and shakes his head. "That doesn't make sense. If someone has closed their fist, why would I see it as open?"

"Love never makes sense in war," I say. "Right now, you're emotions are at war. You know you care for Pastor Clark, but you are mad at him. He said something that hurt your feelings. I understand that. I just want you to consider that emotions change, but love should be a constant. God is love." I caress his chin while he's looking at me starry-eyed.

"You were made because your Creator loved you and continued to love you. Everything about you was formed in love. So, like Ernest Lee said, 'When we hate, we are fighting who we are more than the object of our hatred.' Everyone was born to smile, and everyone was born to live with an open fist. See people as they were intended to be, even if they are not. You might just help show them the truth of who they really are."

Shaw stares at me for a moment and says, "Wow! I didn't know I was talking to Gandhi."

"I'm no Gandhi, but I have been using my time in this bed to think this over. Don't you care about Pastor Clark?"

His eyes roll around as if he's watching someone riding a rollercoaster. "Yeah. I do."

"So, what are you going to do about the tension between you two?"

"Me?" he asks. "He's the pastor. He ought to know better."

The door suddenly opens, and Jakes appears. "Did someone call for a cab?"

"Hey, Jakes," I say. "You got here quick."

"Yeah," he says, "I've been waiting for you to get out of here." Jakes, watching me stand up, walks towards my black duffel bag. "I'll grab this."

"Thanks," I say. My grin must be covering my face, because Shaw springs up and over to the bag, grabbing the handle.

"I can get it," he says, struggling to lift it off the ground. "What's in this bag—bricks?"

"Clothes and some other things, but it's probably my school books that are weighing it down," I say.

Jakes obviously gets frustrated with Shaw's pitiful attempt to handle the bag, because he says, "It's pretty heavy, even for me. Maybe I should get that for you."

"I can get it," Shaw says, without even looking up.

When Jakes looks at me, he sees me shaking my head. He shifts his eyes between Shaw and me and silently asks if we are dating. I just raise my eyebrow. He nods slowly and smiles. "Okay then, Shaw," Jakes says. "It's all yours."

If Shaw's point is to prove how interested he is in me, he wins. His skinny arms are trembling as he carries the bag down the long hallways, stairs, and out to the car. He looks like he is going to pass out, but he makes it to Brayden's Mustang without any help. Getting it into the trunk is another story. With Shaw's arms shaking from fatigue, he is barely able to hold the bag off the ground. Both Jakes and I see the sweat on Shaw's face and neck seeping through his cardigan.

Without asking, Jakes grabs the other end, helping Shaw lift the black bag into the trunk.

Except for Jakes asking if I am okay when I get in the car, we ride in relative silence. He is looking in the rearview mirror intently. I'm sure he's glancing at Shaw. It's not until I look in my side mirror back at Shaw and see him staring at Jakes that my assumption is confirmed. In the silence, I lean my head on the window, closing my eyes.

Once we make our way onto I-85, Jakes says, "So, Shaw, who are you?" My eyes open.

"What do you mean?" Shaw asks.

"Tell me about yourself. Who is Shaw?"

"Well, I'm a Pre-Law major at Charlotte University."

"Are you from Charlotte?" Jakes asks.

"No, I'm from Chicago," Shaw says.

"What brought you down here?"

"Like Brayden, my father went to Charlotte University, so it was kind of expected I would too. But I like Charlotte. It's a nice blend of country and city. Are you from Charlotte?"

"All of my life," Jakes says. "This is all I know, and I love it. Even my blood is Carolina Blue." The brief moment of laughter is followed by an awkward silence. "So, Brayden is my brother."

"Yeah," Shaw says, "he talks about you all the time."

"I wasn't done," Jakes says. I glance at Shaw in the mirror. The expression of shock is chiseled into his face. "You seem like a cool dude, so I want to like you. Just don't get it twisted. If you ever hurt him, you will answer to me. Got it?"

I can hear Shaw gulp like he's in pain. "Yeah."

"Good," Jakes says. "Very good."

§§§§§

Jakes and Shaw continue to converse until we arrive on the campus.

"We're here," Jakes says, tapping me after I doze off for a few minutes. "It's time to put on your game face. Coach wants to meet with you now."

"What does he want?" I ask.

"Who knows? It's Coach, remember?"

"Oh, I remember." As we drive into the school's roundabout, I can't help but think of my father when I see the statue of Martin Luther King, Jr. in the middle.

"Aren't you glad to be back?" Shaw asks.

I breathe deep and say, "I'll know soon." Looking ahead, I can see the tree where my father kissed my mother. A single tear pushes out from my right eye and rolls down my warm cheek. As my ability to see the tree is hindered by the black Navigator we just parked next too, I'm snapped from my emotional trance. "I guess this is it, huh?"

"It's going to be all good, bro," Jakes says. "Are you coming in too, Shaw?"

"Yep," Shaw says, reaching his hand over the seat and on to my shoulder. He squeezes gently. "I wouldn't rather be anywhere else."

"Well, come on then you two," Brayden says. "The quicker we get this over with, the sooner you can get back to your room." Shaw gets out of the backseat fast enough to shut his door and open mine.

"Thank you," I say.

He smiles and winks his eye. "It's my pleasure."

I stop when we arrive at the green metal doors.

"What's wrong," Shaw asks.

"It's been a while since I have seen these doors."

Jakes steps beside me and says, "Well, get used to them again, because you will be seeing a lot more of them."

"We will see," I say.

Jakes taps me on the back. "Coach says that your words shape your world, so think and speak positively. You might be surprised by the outcome."

I shrug my shoulders and walk through the door that Shaw is holding open. When I walk in, I hear Coach's whistle blow.

"One more!" After Coach screams, I hear the sound of feet thundering and balls bouncing against the hardwood floor. Once Coach sees us, he waves. When I approach, Coach opens his arms. "Come here, Foster." If confusion weren't holding my mind hostage like a band of pirates, I would be focused on the pain that Coach's bear hug is inflicting on my sore body. "It's good to have you back, son."

"Thanks, Coach," I say.

Coach lets go of his hug, which felt more like a wrestling hold and folds his arm. "I see that Heart took good care of you."

"Yeah, I can't really say the same for you or the rest of the team. Why didn't you ever come?"

Coach turns pale and nearly chokes on his tongue. "Uh...you know...I was—"

"He was growing," a familiar voice says behind me.

When I turn around, Pastor Clark is standing there. "What are you doing here?" I ask.

"Hello, Brayden. Hello, Jakes. Hello, Shaw. It's good to see you all," Pastor Clark says, as he grins and walks beside Coach. "Coach Bridge is a member of my church. When you mentioned your team affiliation, I was expecting to see him one day at the hospital. We know that didn't happen. So, I made a mental note to converse with him once I left." Pastor Clark places his hand on Coach's shoulder. "Our discourse was extremely productive. Now, are we going to get started? Tomorrow is Sunday, and I have an essential sermon to finish."

Coach grabs his whistle and blows it until he turns purple. "Come on in men. I want two lines!" My other ten teammates stop and form lines facing each other. "Okay, we want to take a moment and welcome back Foster." The teammates look at Coach, each other and then me before they start clapping. Their hesitation is as apparent as my stitches. I still nod and smile.

"We know that Foster endured a regrettable situation, but, by standing here today, he has proven that he has the true heart of a Hornet: strength, endurance, and determination. Now, before we get back to practice, I need to introduce our special guest, my pastor, Pastor Clark." I join everyone else as they clap. "He wants to say a few words, so give him your attention and the same respect you give me. Pastor Clark…"

Pastor Clark takes a few steps forward to center himself between the two lines. "Good day. I'm happy to be here with Coach Bridge. This team should feel honored to be guided by such an exceptional leader and an honorable man. My affection and respect for him is not an obligation because he is a member of my church; it is the truth. Let us take a moment and acknowledge Coach Bridge for his efforts towards excellence on and off the court."

After everyone finishes clapping, Coach says, "I pay him to say those kinds of things, so don't clap too loud. He's going to be expecting a raise." When I see Pastor Clark cover his mouth in laughter, I can't help but laugh as well.

"You're a good man, Coach." He faces the team again. "Today, I am actually not here for Coach Bridge. I'm here for Brayden."

"Huh," I say.

"You are aware that Brayden was assaulted two weeks ago, and none of you are ignorant of the key factor that led to such brutality. My purpose for being here is twofold. The first reason I am here is to encourage you to support Brayden in these weeks and months to come. Unless one of you have encountered a similar situation, I am certain that none of us know the detriment that is deeper than any physical scar. So, spend some time with him, help him if he is in need, and, for those of you who do so, pray with and for him as often as you can."

Pastor Clark looks at Coach Bridge and nods his head. Coach then walks outside. "The second reason I am present is to ensure that the parties responsible for these heinous actions are reprimanded appropriately."

One of the teammates asks, "What do you want with us?"

"Is it not obvious what I am implying?" Pastor Clark asks. All but two of the teammates look around. I find myself staring at Terrance and Dan—who are standing across from one another. "Some of you may remember Spencer Heart, Jakes Heart's brother. I remember him well, because, about two years ago, I was assigned the unfortunate task of administering his eulogy. What I find interesting are the identical elements found in Spencer and Brayden's beatings."

The metal doors open again, and a police officer walks into the gym with Coach.

Pastor resumes talking to get everyone's attention back on him. "Don't mind him. Since it is evident that the people involved have a predilection for violence, I invited some members of my church who happen to be officers in the Charlotte Police Department. So, where was I? Oh, yes, there were identical elements in both beatings. Both were athletes on this team, both identified as same gender loving men, and both were taken into the same field. The only difference is that one actually lived. Brayden, will you be so kind as to come here for a moment."

With Terrance staring at me, I step to Pastor Clark's side.

"Brayden?" Pastor Clark says.

"Yessir?"

"I have one simple question for you: Who attacked you?"

Before I can even point, Dan sprints towards the hallway opposite of Coach and the officer. Halfway to the door leading to the exit, another officer appears. Dan begins scurrying around the room like a roach when lights are turned on. He looks at Terrance, who is now backing away from the other teammates.

"It was you?" Jakes says, running towards Dan.

"Wait!" Dan replies. He attempts to run from Jakes, but his speed is no match for the star of the team. When Jakes tackles him, Dan's face soon slams into the gym floor. Dan's face soon meets Jakes' fists, and Jakes' fists get acquainted with Dan's blood. Soon, the other teammates were adding their own signature attacks. Pastor Clark begins shouting for the team to stop, but no one is listening to the pastor anymore.

Meanwhile, Terrance decides that if he is going to get caught he might as well go out with a bang. The problem is that bang involves me. He charges me like a bull. Just as he is about to make contact, Pastor Clark pushes me out of the way and takes the blunt force of the blow to his side. As both of them crash to the floor, Pastor Clark screams in pain. Before I can ask for help, another officer is grabbing Terrance, flipping him over and locking his wrists in handcuffs.

"Stay down!" the officer says in Terrance's ear. He moves over to Pastor Clark and extends his hand to help him up. When I get a glimpse of the officer's face, he looks familiar.

"Thanks, Terry," Pastor Clark says, holding his side as he stands to his feet.

"Are you okay?" Terry asks.

"I'm fine. Right now, I'm worried about getting that other guy safely into custody."

"I'll handle it," Terry says, dashing to the mound of guys now on Dan. "The next guy that hits him is going to be able to tell all their friends that they know what a taser feels like." Most of the teammates stop immediately, but Derrick and Roderick keep kicking Dan. I don't know much about Terry, but I can tell from his face that isn't joking. Derrick and Roderick find that out too—the hard way. Terry looks back over at Pastor Clark and says, "See, I handled it."

Pastor Clark shakes his head as he rubs his side.

§§§§§

CHAPTER 15: OLIVER CLARK, JR.

Letting Go of the Stone

∞ ∞ ∞

"This is Dan 'da Church Man' Graham, and it's 8 a.m. That's right." I slap the top of the alarm so hard that it slides from under my hand and falls to the floor. "All of you early morning saints that are getting up for your Sunday service, it's time to rise and shine. I'm about to bring you the Sunday mix that will give you more life than your morning brew on Power 88."

I position the alarm clock back on my nightstand and turn off the alarm. Sitting there—alone—on the edge of the king-size bed, I cannot help but wish today's message was unnecessary. I fall back, staring at the white ceiling made black from the darkness in the room.

No sleep.

The alarm did sound, but it didn't awaken me. My mind and body have been alert all night. Typically, I fall fast asleep moments after my head encounters a pillow, but last night was different. Thoughts tracked endlessly through the fields of my mind like the Energizer bunny. After lying in this bed for eight hours, my mind is now blank. All that is left is fear.

I smell bacon.

Sitting up, I slide on my slippers to head downstairs. When I open the door, I can faintly hear the sound of grease sizzling. An amalgamation of breakfast smells greet me as I take the final step. While my face scrunches in confusion, my nostrils flare in anticipation.

I am hungry.

The word 'hunger' may minimize the void I feel in me, for I am hungry even when I am full. This hunger pains me in my mind and soul. I long for my wife and son. I am desperate for them. My existence seems incomplete, knowing they are disconnected from me. So, as I step past my study and hear humming, I feel a part of me become instantly whole. I walk to the kitchen in disbelief. There she is—my angel, my wife—cooking.

Rachel must hear me deeply inhale because she looks over her shoulder. When I see her eyes flicker with delight, I say, "Hey, sunshine."

Grease splatters as she drops the spatula in the pan and says, "Hey, moonshine." She turns her attention back towards the food but positions her hands on the sides of the stove. I strut behind her, placing my hand on her shoulder. Whirling her unsuspecting body around towards me, I stare into her eyes only a moment before pressing my lips against hers. Lost in our embrace, all of my fears vanish. The embers of my soul are rekindling into a supernova of love.

It is not until she smells bacon burning that she loosens her grip on my neck. She meets resistance from me, as she tries to pull back. She twists her head to the side and places her hand on my chest. "Hey, it's going to burn," she says, gently tapping my chest. I let her go and step back until my rear touches the edge of the countertop.

"I missed you," I say.

"Did you really miss me, or did you just miss my cooking?"

"Oh, I missed you." As Rachel flips the bacon, I am reticent. What do I say? For minutes, I stand there, speechless. "I know I do not deserve you."

"Let's just eat, Oliver," she says. "I'm here. You're here. So, let's eat. Okay?"

"Okay."

I walk into the dining room and find the table already set. "Just have a seat," Rachel says. "I'm almost done."

I sit down, attempting to utilize the time to organize my thoughts. My efforts seem futile, because, after ten minutes pass, I am no closer to a concise verbal expression of my sentiments. When Rachel walks in with the food, I smile and offer to pull out her chair.

"Just sit and enjoy your meal," she says, sitting down.

"It smells delicious, Rachel."

"Thank you." She grabs my plate and fills it with food: boiled eggs, grits, pancakes, and crisp bacon. Setting the plate in front of me, Rachel takes her own and does the same. She asks me to pray for the food. After I do, she says, "Eat up."

We eat through our food, offering occasional glances at one another. After feeling a spring of tension gushing up in me, I say, "I appreciate the meal, Rachel. I really do. But, are we going to talk about—you know what?"

"Are you sure you want to do that before your first Sunday back at church?" Rachel asks.

"Yes. I want to give space for us to discuss it."

Rachel situates her fork on the plate. "Okay. Where do I begin? For the last two weeks, I have felt completely helpless in this situation, like a rubber duck in a whirlpool. You made me feel that way. I was hurting Oliver. I wanted to make you hurt, so I took Oli with me. That's why I didn't come to visit you in the hospital."

"So, what brought you—" I begin.

"Let me finish," she says, holding up her pointer finger. "I wanted you to feel what I was feeling. It hurt to be away from you, leaving you alone at such a sensitive time. I was in a dark place. All the while, I kept hearing the words that Gloria read to me before I left the house: 'Darkness never loved me.' We have some dark days, but when we are on the same page, there is nothing but light. I want that light back." She gestures to me. "You can talk now."

I smile and say, "I do too."

"Well, what are we going to do?" she asks, looking into my eyes.

"I want you and Oli home. I promise I will do what it takes to make that happen."

"Your promises have fallen pretty flat recently."

"I know. I haven't been too proud of my decisions, but I was a different person."

Rachel shakes her head and says, "Oliver, I wouldn't buy that if it was free."

"Why do you say that?" I ask.

"You can't tell me you were a different person. You were you. Alcohol or no alcohol, you make the decisions, so I won't let you just pass the blame off to some convenient alter ego."

"Okay. Let me rephrase that."

"No. Don't rephrase it," she says, tapping my arm. "Don't repackage and try to resend it. Just save it. You said you want to have a discussion. Let's keep it real if we are going to do it."

I clear my throat. "I am sorry."

"Ding. Ding. Ding." Rachel says, leaning back in her chair. "Now we are getting somewhere. Proceed."

"Well, I am sorry."

"Ding. Sorry. there is just something special about those three words."

"You aren't making this easy, Rachel," I say, "but, I can imagine that I have not made your life entirely easy these last few months."

"Ding. Okay, that was the last one in me."

"Could you ever love me like you used to?" I ask.

"I never stopped loving you, Oliver. There were days I prayed that God would take the love I have for you away, but God never did. I realized something: since God is love, God can't remove love, because God would be taking away a piece of Himself from us. Now, it is up to me to stay with you or not."

"So, you decided to stay?" I ask, leaning forward.

"At first, no. I didn't. In fact, it wasn't until last night, when I found out what you did at the school, that I decided that maybe you did deserve another chance."

"How did you find out about that?"

"Gloria. You know us girls have to stick together," Rachel says, laughing.

"I see. Well, if that helped, then I'm glad she did tell you."

"You better. I only have one question, and you know what it is: are you still drinking?"

"Rachel," I say, extending my hand, "No. I haven't even used Listerine for fear of the alcohol content."

"I know I'm joking with you, but I am serious."

"I am just as serious. This time I have a plan. I'm working with Terry to restart my A.A. meetings. I won't be hiding anything from you. In fact, I want to know if you would be willing to join me at some of my meetings."

"Really? You want me to go?" she asks.

"You aren't just a part of my world. You are my world."

She places her hand in mine and squeezes. "I love you, Oliver."

"I love you more."

"Well," she says, cleaning the damp space under her eyes, "I know I said I only had one question, but I have one more."

"Okay, dear. Go for it. I'm on a roll."

"Are we going to have to find another church after today's message?"

"Why is that?" I ask.

"I know you," she says. "You don't bite your tongue in these types of situations."

"My love, whatever happens, if you are by my side, I know that my unknown destiny will be greater than my fear of the unknown."

"See," Rachel says, "telling me things like that is how you tricked me into marrying you."

"Oh, it was a trick now?" I ask.

"Well, Halloween is a few weeks away. Why don't you show me whether it was a trick or a treat?"

"What do you have in mind?"

"Well, I cooked something up downstairs. Let's see if you can cook something upstairs?"

"What about Gloria and Nahlia?" I ask.

"I made enough food for the entire house. You just see if you can get it right with me."

She pushes away from the table and sprints towards the stairs. The chase ensues, and the king-size bed is full once more.

§§§§§

The congregation erupts with cheers and applause when I step into the sanctuary with Rachel. Even with the microphone, the minister that is up reading the announcements is muffled by the sound of over seven thousand people bestowing upon me a humbling expression of love. I stop and wave to the congregation. Trying to maintain my composure, I resume walking to my chair on the pulpit.

The minister makes a passionate speech about being glad I am back, before returning to the announcements. The rest happens to be a blur. The dancers perform, and the choir sings. Meanwhile, my mind is elsewhere.

When it is time for me to approach the podium, I do so with excitement. "Good morning, family. It is good to be home!" I wait a few moments for the congregation to settle down from their enthusiasm. "I am excited about today's message, so you will have to forgive me for bypassing some of the usual pleasantries that I give during my pastoral remarks. I am going to be reading from the King James Version of the Bible. Please turn with me to the eighth chapter of John, and I will commence reading at the first verse of scripture and conclude at the eleventh."

[1]Jesus went unto the Mount of Olives. [2]And early in the morning he came again into the temple, and all the people came unto him; and he sat down, and taught them. [3]And the scribes and Pharisees brought unto him a woman taken in adultery; and when they had set her in the midst, [4]they say unto him, Master, this woman was taken in adultery, in the very act. [5]Now Moses in the law commanded us, that such should be stoned: but what sayest thou? [6]This they said, tempting him that they might have to accuse him. But Jesus stooped down, and with his finger wrote on the ground, as though he heard them not. [7]So when they

continued asking him, he lifted up himself, and said unto them, He that is without sin among you, let him first cast a stone at her. ⁸And again he stooped down, and wrote on the ground. ⁹And they which heard it, being convicted by their own conscience, went out one by one, beginning at the eldest, even unto the last: and Jesus was left alone, and the woman standing in the midst. ¹⁰When Jesus had lifted up himself, and saw none but the woman, he said unto her, Woman, where are those thine accusers? Hath no man condemned thee? ¹¹She said, No man, Lord. And Jesus said unto her, neither do I condemn thee: go, and sin no more.

"My title and relevant question are the same today, so if you would, turn to your neighbor and ask them this one thing: How do I let go of this stone?" With voices blending from all over the sanctuary, the congregation sounds like they are mumbling, as they repeat the words I presented to them.

I lean back, take a deep breath, and begin. "I have studied and preached from this passage of text before. In those times of reflecting on this scripture, I was left with conflicting emotions. On the one hand, I wanted to be upset with the Pharisees for humiliating this woman, bringing her naked body before a crowd of people. On the other hand, she was caught in adultery, which is a sin etched in stone tablets we call the Ten Commandments. It deserves punishment. On the one hand, I wanted to feel sorry for her, and, on the other, I wanted to judge her. There was a brewing dichotomy of perspectives bubbling inside of me."

"I came to realize the reason I was so conflicted about her was that I was conflicted about me. Soon, I was seeing this message in a different light, and I was able to answer the question that I asked you to pose to your neighbor: How do I let go of this stone? I would be remiss if I simply gave you the answer but did not explain the duality of stoning."

"First you have the one about to be stoned—the adulterer. We don't know this woman's name. Her political, social, and economic status is a mystery. We are not informed to whom she is married. All we know is that her sin is singled out. Throughout your life, you will encounter people who are ready to stone you. For whatever reason, they will come to you ready to kill you. They may not kill you in the literal sense, but they might as well if they destroy your purpose, destiny, and future. They might as well kill you if they refuse to exercise the grace that is now accessible to you."

"When Adam ate from the forbidden tree, he was expelled from the Garden of Eden, because there was no system of grace in place. When God was fed up with the sin of the people, God sent a massive flood, because there was no system of grace in place. When God burned Sodom and Gomorrah, there was no overarching system of grace in place. If there were no system in place today, your best attempt at being holy, righteous, and perfect would still be seen as a filthy rag to God. The choir would be grounded from the garden. The pastors would be caught up in a flood. Everyone in this church, including me, would burn up in the fires of Sodom."

"But, thanks be unto God, who has given us the free gift of grace through Jesus Christ. Romans 5:15 tells us that 'if through the offense of one many be dead, much more the grace of God, and the gift of grace, which is by one man, Jesus Christ, hath abounded unto many.' Basically, Jesus' presence represents the incalculable possibilities of God's grace afforded to us."

"By now, some might think I am making excuses for sin, but I am merely doing what Jesus did in this text: neither condoning the act nor condemning the person. Maybe you had a child out of wedlock or contracted an STD. Maybe you have been keeping secrets and lying to those you love, or maybe you are just like this woman—caught in the very act of your sin. What you did is wrong, but you are never wrong. You are right because of God's unyielding love for you. Romans 5:8 reveals that God shows love towards us by dying for us while we were still in sin. It's easy to love perfect people, but God came to love imperfect people perfectly. Somebody ought to tell somebody: You are loved."

I take a sip of water resting under the podium, as the congregation roars from saying those words with passion.

"Now, we must look at the other side of the stone—the person getting ready to cast it—we must be aware of God's heart. In Jeremiah 29:11, God declares, 'I know the thoughts I have for you, plans to prosper you and not to harm you, plans to give you hope and a future.' We are also told in John 3:17 that 'God did not send his Son into the world to condemn the world, but to save the world through him.' With that in mind, I am left bewildered that these religious authorities do not display more compassion with this woman."

"Instead, these religious authorities come to Jesus ready to tell him what must be done with this sinner. We believe that Jesus is God in the flesh. Therefore, when we reread this, we see men who act like they have mastered the thoughts and ideas of God coming to God to tell God what God should do based on what they believe God would do. They tell Jesus that to fulfill God's will—through the Law of Moses—Jesus must agree that this woman should be stoned."

"Like anyone wanting to stone you, it's a trap. The problem with executing the Law of Moses at this time is that the Romans are occupying the land. As the ruling system over this nation, they have decreed that Jews cannot perform these executions. So, if Jesus agrees to her stoning, they will turn him into the Roman authorities. If he disagrees with stoning her, then he will be accused of breaking Moses' Law. They put Jesus in this situation to trap and trick him, using a system of stoning."

"There are people in your life right now with a complicated, hypocritical system set up to stone you when you do something they disagree with. What I find interesting is how confident these people are. They will bring an adulterous woman before Jesus, coming to him as leopards attempting to point out the spots of others. In Luke 6:42, Jesus asks the Pharisees how it is that they can tell someone else to take a speck out of their eye when they aren't able to see the log in their own.

I grew up in church, so I remember the mothers of the church would be seen as pillars of holiness. They were always fasting and praying. Over time, I have seen these same mothers gossip, lie, and even commit adultery. I am only using them as an example to denote that even the holiest among us, including me, aren't perfect. In fact, Isaiah 64:6 tells us that we are all unclean, and our righteousness is like a filthy rag."

"So, when the Pharisees decry this woman's sin, it is not surprising that Jesus seemingly ignores them, bends down, and begins writing on the ground. This is why the Creator is not alarmed when we hit rock bottom. God made the rock."

The congregation breaks out in praise. People are jumping up and clapping, shouting, "I know that's right."

"God knows your rocky moments. Not only does God know your sin, but God has also freed you from that sin. However, there are Pharisees in your life waiting to find someone to throw a stone at, and it just so happened that this woman fell in their line of sight. They might not have been out to get her specifically, but they were looking to stone someone. People who want to cast stones will do so regardless of who it is and what it costs, even if it costs a life. Like the Pharisees, they will step right in the face of God and demand that God deal with you. In fact, they are so bold that they don't find rocks at God's feet, but they bring their own to use against you."

"Today, stoning is a primitive and brutal form of punishment; however, during the era of this text, it is strangely rational. Personal vendettas are defused by stoning. Everyone in the community is given a stone and told to throw it at the adulterers so that it is the community doing it and not an individual. This is why preachers and politicians want you to rally against something. They can't stone alone. They need a community. So, when the Pharisees come to Jesus, they are upholding this thought, with one exception: it is personal."

"I mentioned earlier that the Pharisees are attempting to trap Jesus. This woman is merely caught in the crossfire of their scheme. The reason they carry a stone and the reason they want to stone her are the same—it is personal. That's right. It's personal! When people are adamant about seeing you go down for what you did, it is because there is a part in them working tirelessly to cover up their own missteps and misdeeds. It's personal. They want you to pay because it's personal. They won't stop seeking your demise. That's personal. The more stones they get people to throw at you, the fewer stones that can get thrown in their direction."

"It's personal because the stone they are throwing is more about them than the person they are casting it towards. That is why Jesus' simple phrase, 'He that is without sin among you, let him first cast a stone at her,' struck a nerve in them that was so piercing they walked away. It's easy to throw a stone when you feel no one knows your fault, but it is much more difficult when your sin is known.

Your judgment loses its significance. Your defamation of character loses its' power. That's why Jesus tells us in Luke 6:37, 'Do not judge and you will not be judged. Do not condemn, and you will not be condemned. Forgive, and you will be forgiven.'"

"That is the answer to the question I posed earlier: How do I let go of this stone? If you are looking to stone someone else with judgment, consider the judgment you can receive. If you are thinking of condemning someone, remember the condemnation you deserve. If none of that works just remember that the wages of sin are death. Consider the grace of God that you cling to so confidently. It takes an ample amount of forgiveness to cover your grievances. It would be a terrible thing if the forgiveness needed in your life were revoked due to a lack of forgiveness found in your heart."

"Church, it is time for us that have stoned so many in our church and community to remember the sweet sound of God's amazing grace that can still save wretches like you and me. We were once lost, but in God's grace, we are found. We were blind, but now, through the light of God's love, we can see. Now that we know the power of God's grace and the permanence of God's love, we who are aware of these free gifts are called to let go of our stones, throw open our arms, and embrace those who are still lost without love."

§§§§§

CHAPTER 16: BRAYDEN FOSTER

A Stone in the Rock

∞ ∞ ∞

Pastor Clark begins to step down from the podium. While motioning to Shaw, he says, "Paul writes in Romans chapter eight that 'if God be for us, who can be against us.'"

Gloria leans over to me and asks, "Who is Paul?"

"He is one of the authors of the New Testament."

"Oh, okay," she says, returning to her original position. I watch as her focus becomes glued to the front. I take for granted how many people didn't grow up with this church life. When I look back, Shaw is bringing out a large stone and handing it to Pastor Clark.

"This," Pastor Clark says, "is the sin stone that is given to me." He lifts the stone over his head. "As you can see, it is pretty big. Honestly, it should be bigger, but if it were, I wouldn't be able to lift it." I hear Nahlia and Terry joining in with many in the congregation who are laughing. "I am serious. Can you imagine how much the sin of your entire life weighs if just one equals death? You must answer that for yourself. Just notice what happened; this stone was handed to me. Shaw just acted like the Pharisees, giving me a stone. Now, he would have been throwing it in that age, but he knows better."

I lean over to Gloria and say, "He is kind of funny."

"Honey, just don't tell him that," she says, shaking her head.

When I look again, Shaw is making his way out with a black metal container on a rolling cart. He stops right in front of Pastor Clark and stands to the side.

"They give me this rock because they believe that God's grace is so fragile that a particular sin can keep me from God's love and grace," Pastor continues.

Crash!

"Mom, what did Pastor Clark just do?" Nahlia asks Gloria as the crowd gasps.

"He just threw the stone in the box," Gloria replies.

"Why?"

"You have to wait and find out," Gloria says.

"Based on the expectations of Pharisees," Pastor Clark says, "that is my sin meeting God's grace—it shatters. It is not strong enough to handle the weight of my sin. So now, I am left with broken pieces of God's grace." He motions to Shaw, and Shaw grabs the cart and rolls the container out of the sanctuary. "Why not commit suicide? Why not end it all if God's grace isn't enough to handle what I've already done? I can't tell you what I will do, but I know that if God grants me another 40 plus years of life, I will make another mistake. If God's grace is this weak, what is the point of going forward when I will only make more of God's grace shatter?"

The room grows so silent. I watch as Pastor digs his hand into his pocket and pulls out something that seems to fit right in the palm of his hand.

"This is my stone," Pastor Clark says. "If I'm a Pharisee, me carrying this stone around may be necessary because I'm ready to stone you. But if I would be honest, the real reason this stone stays with me is a deep desire to stone myself. I know that doesn't make you shout when I say that, but I must be authentic. No one walks around with the weight of a stone without them really wanting to stone themselves. This stone is really my sin stone. Throwing it at you just momentarily releases my mind from the guilt of my own sin."

"Wow," Terry says, "that's good stuff."

"Yeah," I say.

"Oh, did you hear that?"

"Hear what?" I ask.

"My stomach. I can't wait to eat," Terry says, patting his stomach.

Acting like I didn't hear him, I turn my attention back to Pastor Clark. He says, "If I am the adulterous woman, the only reason I do not have a stone is that I'm naked. My nakedness doesn't take away the fact that I really want to stone myself. So, you have leaders bringing me to Jesus. They want to stone themselves, but they are so proud and arrogant with their assumed knowledge of God that they would rather stone me. I want to stone myself, but they wouldn't even let me grab a stone on the way to Jesus."

Pastor Clark motions to Shaw again, and he wheels out a massive rock that looks like it's been cut out in the middle.

"Mom, I like the front much better," Nahlia says.

"This front row thing is a bit too much," Gloria says, "but I do like being closer."

Pastor Clark says, "People who want to stone themselves want to stone me because hurt people hurt people. They live like their positions in the church will save them, but, in their hearts, they are as scared as this adulterous woman is at this moment. I am sure that many of you are wondering why I asked the ushers and greeters to pass out small stones to everyone on the way in. We all have sin stones. Today, I want to illustrate that none of you, from the pulpit to the parking lot, are exempt from the need of the rock of salvation." He points down to the rock in front of him.

He gets quiet for a moment. "I am not an adulterer, but I know drunkenness." The air seems to get thin. "Yes, your Pastor isn't perfect. Again, I am not condoning what I have done, but I also realize that I am not condemned because of it.

A slow clap turns into a cavalcade of applause. "I wanted to throw stones at myself. I wanted to run and hide, but my loving wife, with her patience, forgiveness, and love, has shown me grace beyond measure. I want to thank the others who have played a part in reminding me of God's love and abounding grace. They know who they are. They came into my life in such unexpected ways, but they have changed the way my heart beats for others. It wasn't until I was assured that God loved me that I could embrace the love waiting all around me."

"Now, I am certain there are some of you who feel unlovable like you don't deserve God's love or forgiveness. Maybe you still feel like stoning yourself, due to the mistakes you have made in the course of your life. I want you to bring your stone and step into the aisle. I don't care who you are or what you may have done. Pharisee and adulterer alike, come with your stone."

I see people flocking to the aisles to line up. Many of their eyes are filled with tears, and they are clutching their stones tightly. When Nahlia stands up with Gloria, they begin walking towards the aisle. Gloria turns back around and looks at me. It's like she is communicating with me telepathically to get in line.

I stand just as Pastor Clark says, "Paul writes in Romans chapter 8 that 'if God be for us, who can be against us.' God is for you, neither condoning nor condemning your actions. God is for you because God loves you."

Pastor leans over to Shaw and whispers something in his ear. Shaw looks in my direction. He walks over to the front and tells all of us to come to Pastor Clark. Coach Bridge and the basketball team, Gloria and Nahlia, Terry, Pastor's wife, and I step in front of Pastor Clark.

Pastor Clark says, "People often write others off because of where they are in their lives and what they do, but I have come to see for myself that God is in the hospital just like God is in the holy church. Hold up your stones."

We all lift up our stones.

"You all are from different backgrounds, and you stand here for different reasons. However, one of the things you share in common is God's about to handle your stone. Mary and Martha thought they would need to move the stone blocking Jesus' tomb, but when they arrived, it was already removed. By the time they tried to handle the stone, God, the Rock, already moved it. This rock before you represents God, the rock on which our faith is built upon. As a symbol of God's ability to handle your stone, I am going to ask you to place your stone in this rock. God's grace won't fail, and it won't break. As you put your stone down, know you are loved, and that all the guilt and shame you have been holding on to has been overshadowed by God's love and grace."

Pastor Clark motioned for us to lay down our stones. The basketball team threw in their stones and stepped back. Three of my teammates were crying like they were at a funeral. Coach chucked his stone in the rock and went over to hug those three guys. The other teammates huddled around them. Coach began to pray. I didn't know what he was saying, but I just knew he was praying. I never heard him pray before, so I wanted to throw my stone in and dash over to them.

When I turned back towards the rock, all I could do was stare at it. Nahlia gently placed her stone down. I could tell Gloria's gaze just shifted from Nahlia to me. She places her hand on the small of my back.

"Do it with me," Gloria says to me.

I lift my arm over the rock and allow the stone to slip from my moist hand. I hear our stones as they crash against the rock and other stones already in there.

The stone is so small, but, as it leaves my hand, it feels like the weight of the world has shifted off of my shoulders. My new weightlessness is marked by the tears that feel like they are spraying from my eyes like geysers.

Gloria turns and embraces me. Her touch reminds me of my mother's and causes me to cry harder. Every time I try to stop crying, I hear Gloria and Nahlia crying with me. It only pushes out more tears. I feel like they are crying for me, as I am crying for them.

§§§§§

CHAPTER 17: OLIVER CLARK, JR.

Love Above All Else

∞ ∞ ∞

"Terry, the food is ready," Rachel says, stepping into the living room.

"What no one else is supposed to eat?" I ask.

"Now, Oliver," Rachel says, "you know that if I don't get Terry a plate, he will go around the city telling people we let him starve when he comes over."

"Besides," Terry says, "I'm a grown man. I have to eat a healthy meal."

"So, what am I then, Terry?" I ask.

"You're just Junior," he says, getting up from the sofa and heading towards the kitchen. He turns back and looks at everyone in the room, "If you don't want your food, just let me know." He steps out and pokes his head back in. "Oh, and, not coming to the table after I sit down means you don't want your food."

"Ugh!" Gloria says. "Who does he think he is? What a rude, inconsiderate—"

"Mom…" Nahlia says, looking up with her head in her mother's lap.

"She must be ungry, Nahlia," I say.

Gloria snaps, "I am. I don't want him to eat all the food."

"Nahlia, I am going to have to agree with your mother on this one," I say. "Terry does not joke much when it comes to food."

"Yeah," Brayden says, "he was even talking about food during your message."

"No surprise there," I say, standing up. "Well, I hope all of you are hungry enough to pull away from the Panther's whooping up on the Buccaneers and join us in the dining room."

"I'm tempted to stay," Brayden says. "This is one of the few times I get to see them beating anyone."

"Just for that, I am going to give Terry permission to eat your portion of food," I say.

Brayden stands up and says, "I'm pretty sure he doesn't need any permission to do that."

"You know," I say, chuckling, "you're probably right."

As we walk into the dining room, I notice that Rachel and Terry are already seated. "Honey, where would you like everyone to sit?" Rachel asks.

"Let's see. I thought this through a little while ago." I walk around the table and stand at the end. "Rachel and I will sit here. We will place Nahlia and Oli across from one another. Gloria, you will sit across from Terry."

"Umm, do I have to sit there?" Gloria asks.

"It's just dinner, Gloria," I say.

"Hey, what's the big deal?" Terry asks. "You afraid I might eat all your food?"

"No," Gloria says. "I'm afraid that I might get sick from looking at you."

"Mom!" Nahlia says, pulling on Gloria's arm.

"Huh? What did I do to you?" Terry asks.

"You just—" Gloria begins.

"Can you two meet me in my study for a moment?" I ask. Gloria stares at me for a moment and swings her silky hair as she struts out of the room.

"Junior, what's the deal?" Terry asks.

"Meet me in my office."

"Okay. I'm going," Terry says, backing out of the room.

Brayden's face shifts from confusion to delight when I say, "Brayden, you will sit across from Shaw."

"That's great," Shaw says, "but that leaves four more plate settings. Are others supposed to be coming?"

"They should be here any minute now," I say.

"I almost forgot about them," Rachel says. "I should have waited until they arrived before I told Terry the food was ready."

"Well, by the time I finish with him and Gloria, our other guests should be here."

"Is it a surprise, Mom?" Oli asks.

"Actually, it is," Rachel replies.

"I don't like surprises," Oli says.

"Oli, son," I say, "Why don't you help your mother put ice in the glasses? Everyone else can take their seats. We will get started momentarily."

"Okay, Dad," Oli says, over the sound of oak chairs moving along the wooden floors, as our guests take their seats.

§§§§§

"But what did I do?" I hear Terry ask, as I walk through my study door.

"You're an—" Gloria begins.

"Hey! Hey! Hey!" I say. "Gloria, what is going on here?"

"That pig is—"

"Gloria," I say, "can we make it through this conversation without reducing ourselves to the playground tactics of name-calling? Why don't we have a seat?" She makes a low moan and plops down in a chair. I walk around the desk to my chair. When Terry is sitting down, Gloria scoots her chair away from him. "Seriously, Gloria, what has Terry done to you that warrants such aggression?"

"Yeah, tell me something," Terry says.

"Terry," I say, "please don't instigate. Gloria, would you mind explaining?"

"He is just like every other man," she says.

"What's that supposed to mean?" Terry asks.

"Terry, would you please let me handle this?" I ask.

"Okay. Okay."

"I'm sorry. Go ahead, Gloria," I say.

"Thank you," Gloria says. "Terry is just like every other man. He came on to me."

"I asked you out on a date!" Terry says.

"Yeah, but you know what you really want," she says.

"What do I really want?"

"You know. I don't have to tell you."

"Gloria, we have guests and food waiting for us—" I begin.

"Amen!" Terry says.

"Terry…" I say.

"I'm sorry. I got a little carried away."

"Gloria," I say, "if we are going to do this now, you need to be upfront about what is bothering you."

"He thinks he wants to go on a date with me, but he doesn't know all of my baggage," Gloria says. "He doesn't know all the things I've done. He doesn't know anything about me."

"You have to give me a chance to get to know you," Terry says.

"What's the point?" Gloria asks. "You won't want me after you find out more about me."

"How can you tell me what I won't like?"

"I just know," she says. "You like what you see on the outside, but you can't handle the things going on inside of me."

"Gloria, you're right. I don't know much about you. All I have is what I see on the outside."

"See. That's so typical," Gloria says, looking at me with her finger pointed at Terry.

"I won't deny you are a beautiful woman, but I see so much more on the outside. I see a strong woman who knows how to raise an amazing daughter despite all odds. You don't back down from a challenge. I can tell because you were willing to move mountains to keep your girl happy. That's on the outside."

"You see all that?" she asks, softening her voice.

"Yeah," Terry says, "I'm a cop, so I see a lot."

"Well, there are some things that only doctors can see."

"Gloria, you don't have to do this," I say.

"He thinks he wants to get to know me," she says. "Let me help him get to know me."

"What am I missing?" Terry asks, switching his gaze between both of us.

"I'm HIV positive," she says, staring at him in his face.

"Umm...okay. I'm sorry to hear that," Terry says as his face scrunches in sadness.

"Is that all you're going to say?" Gloria asks.

"What are you waiting for me to say?" Gloria looks at him. "Did you think I was going to say that you were right and run out of here? I won't say I'm not shocked, but do you really think I'm that fickle?"

"You're a man," she says.

"Yeah, I'm a man," Terry says. "I'm a man who watched breast cancer eat away at my fiancée. I'm a man who stayed by her bedside for six months. I'm a man who sees the same fight in your eyes that I saw in hers, but I'm also a man who won't sit around and be disrespected by a woman who wants to feel sorry for herself."

"How could you say something like that?" Gloria asks, as Terry stands up and walks toward the door.

"When my fiancée was diagnosed, she fought with everything she had. Not one day did she ever question how much time we would have together. We spent every day living life to the fullest. Now, I look at you sitting there rejecting me, because you are afraid to love, afraid to be loved. How many times do you have to read *Unlovable* before you realize how much love is around you?" Terry closes the door as he walks out of the room.

Gloria looks at me, waiting for an answer. "Well?"

"Well, what?" I ask.

"Come on, pastor; you preached a great message this morning about stones. Don't you have anything to tell me now?"

"You know I do," I say, standing up and moving to the chair beside her. "He's right."

"Come on. Really? Is that the best you have? Is that all you're going to tell me?"

"Gloria, you read Ernest Lee's book more times than anyone, and you helped me deal with my own issues. You should be living in the truth that Ernest Lee wrote and that Terry is pointing towards. If not, I am not going to be able to start calling you the relationship guru."

"Well, maybe you should hold off on that title," she says. "It's always easier to give advice than to live advice."

"That is true, but you are able to live it, Gloria."

Gloria looks at me and raises an eyebrow. "You have to say that. You're a pastor."

"I only need to tell you the truth," I say, smiling. "He is right, you know."

Her countenance droops almost as much as her head, as her chin rests against her chest. "I know."

She hesitates a moment; however, when she looks up at me, her pain is evident. "No tears. No tears, Gloria." Looking into her eyes, I feel like her mind is sailing as a toy boat on whitewater rapids. "Gloria..." She is non-responsive. "Gloria!"

"I don't want to," she mutters.

"What don't you want to do?" I ask.

"I don't want to die."

The doorbell rings, and I, instinctively, turn my head as if I can see through my study door. When I face Gloria again, she is already sliding down toward the floor. "Gloria..." I catch her, and we slide down together. My back is now pressing against the oak desk. As her head rests on my thigh, I only know that she is crying by the increased dampness of my slacks. I rub her shoulder, thinking of all the times I've been down on this floor. "Gloria, I know you are scared. Just know you are not alone."

"Bu...bu...but, I'm going to end up like Ernest Lee."

"No, Gloria. You're not," I say. "Ernest Lee gave his life away. You don't have to do that. You can live. After all the great words Ernest Lee wrote for us, he wasn't able to live the advice he gave. He gave up on loving himself. He let his fear of HIV override his joy for love and life. You don't have to do that. He died alone, but you are here—alive—with all of us."

"I'm not going to kill myself; it's going to kill me," she says.

"There are more ways to kill yourself than the way Ernest Lee did. The moment you live in fear, you begin to die." I lift her head up out of my lap. "You have too much to lose not to live."

Few tears flow after my last few phrases, but her face is still filled with fear. "Do you think Terry really likes me?" she asks.

"What I know is that you are far from unlovable."

§§§§§

By the time Gloria and I make it back into the dining room, the doorbell has sounded twice, and all of the guests have arrived. "Sorry for the delay, everyone," I say, letting Gloria step past me to take her seat. Once she glances at the opposite end of the table, her eyes fill with the same bewilderment that is beaming from everyone else's. "I would like to introduce everyone to Coach Bridge and Mr. Foster, Brayden's father." Everyone tries to peel their eyes from the other two visitors that are seated.

"Coach, why don't you take the sit there by Shaw and Mr. Foster, you can take the last seat over there by your son." After they are seated, I walk beside our other gentleman guest and his wife. "It's good to see you both; I'm so glad you could make it."

"I must say, I am humbled by the opportunity for my wife and me to fellowship with your lovely family and friends," he says.

I smile, extending my hand. "You are always welcome, Deacon DuBois." As our courteous handshake concludes, I hear everyone exhale the air they are holding. I take my seat, look straight at him, and smile again. I turn and notice Rachel, who has the distinct pleasure of sitting in front of Mrs. DuBois, is gazing ahead. "I know we are all hungry, so I won't prolong my words."

"Yes," Oli says.

"Oli," Rachel says, giving him the look of sweet death. He leans back in his chair and slaps his hand over his mouth.

As the laughter is subsiding, I say, "I am pleased to welcome all of you. As I look around the room, I see family, friends, former strangers, and foes, but at this table, there is love above all else. Since I feel my beautiful wife pinching my leg, I'm going to allow Deacon DuBois to pray over our meal tonight. Deacon, would you please do the honors?"

"Certainly," he says, clearing his throat. "Let us bow our heads and close our eyes. Our Father—"

As Deacon DuBois prays, I'm laughing to myself, because everyone's eyes are open. Maybe everyone is thinking the same thing my wife said to me earlier when I told her the guest list: "It's much more like a storm brewing in the Gulf not knowing what may come of it."

"Amen." The deacon must be hungry because his prayer is unusually short.

"Amen," I say. "Thank you for that prayer. Everyone enjoy."

I can tell from Brayden's face that he is uncomfortable. After about two minutes of looking in his direction, he locks eyes with me. I wink at him just as Nahlia passes me the green beans. A smile forms on his face, and he nods.

§§§§§

We make it through dinner with light banter. Mr. Foster was quiet and observant, as was Mrs. DuBois. Deacon DuBois was surprisingly garrulous with everyone at the table. Terry and Gloria were doing their best not to look at each other, especially when Coach told the story of how Terry tased his team. Despite being in the midst of all of the interactions, Brayden and Shaw are texting (probably each other) throughout the entire meal. Oli and Nahlia are ready to go back to watching television shortly after finishing their meals, which is fitting since the bulk of the after-dinner dialogue is about Ernest Lee's book.

"Well, I must say, Mrs. Clark, you have outdone yourself with this meal. It was exceptional," Deacon DuBois says, with his wife nodding beside him. "It is getting late, and, as you know, we have an important Deacon's meeting tomorrow. I do want to thank you for your hospitality and everyone else for their company. It's been a pleasure."

I walk to where they are now standing and escort them to the front door. "I'm so glad that you both could come."

"Well, you did say you had an important announcement that would influence my meeting tomorrow," Deacon DuBois says.

"Oh, yes, I do."

"So, what is it?" he asks.

"This," I say, pulling out a folding piece of paper from my pocket.

"What's this?"

"See for yourself," I say, handing it too him. He unfolds the paper and begins reading. Dismay is stuck on his face like superglue on tissue paper.

"This can't be real," he says, glancing at me.

"Keep reading and tell me if those dates are real," I say.

His eyes quint as he scans further down the paper. He looks up into my eyes. "He wouldn't do this to me. He was my friend."

"What is it, darling?" Mrs. DuBois asks.

"I can't believe this," Deacon DuBois says, ignoring his wife's question.

"Yes, he was your friend, but he was my father," I say, opening the front door. "Again, I thank you for gracing our home with your presence. I hope you have a wonderful meeting tomorrow."

"Hmph..." He is shaking, and I can almost see the steam rising from his head. They walk out without another word.

"Pastor," Coach says, startling me.

"Oh, yes, Coach. What is it? Are you leaving too?" I ask.

"Yeah, I'm going to show Mr. Foster how to get back to his hotel room."

"I want to thank you, sir," Mr. Foster says, extending his arm around Coach to shake my hand. "You have really shown my son a great deal of love in my absence." He looks at Brayden. "And I've been very absent."

"Mr. Foster, we are never to underestimate the love of a father. So, with all the love I may have to give, it's your love that matters above all else. I know Brayden loves you and is glad to have you here. Even though you two have a great deal to work through, the fact that you showed up puts you well on your way to a healthy resolution." I turn my focus on Brayden. "Remember, it is a process. You cannot demand that someone change what they believe to be true or false. You can only demand that they love you despite their belief."

I shake hands with Coach and Mr. Foster as they walk out of the open door. Brayden stops in front of me and locks his arms around my waist. "Thank you," is all he says before catching up with his father.

Shaw is right on his heels. "Pastor, I love you," he says, hugging me.

"I love you too, son. Be safe out there, and text me to let me know when you get in."

"Okay. Will do."

I look behind me to make sure no one else is coming before shutting the door.

As I begin to walk away, Terry appears. "You're leaving too?" I ask.

"Yeah, it's about that time, Junior. I'm starting to get the 'itis.'"

"Okay, well, good to see you as always."

"It's good to see you too, bro. You know I'm proud of you, right?" Terry asks.

"Really?"

"Yeah!" Terry says. "You're an inspiration. Even though you never really played sports, you now know what a true comeback is. For that, I'm proud of you."

"Thanks, Terry. You are a true friend."

"No problem. Just remember that on Christmas," he says, laughing and patting me on the back.

After we hug, he gets ready to walk out of the door. "Terry," Gloria says.

"Uh?"

"Can I talk to you for a minute?" she asks.

"I will leave you two to chat. Excuse me," I say, walking past them. When I look back at Terry, I can see that he is fighting a smile."

When I walk into the dining room, I see Rachel carrying dirty plates. "Here sweetheart, let me get that for you," I say, taking them from her hands.

"Thank you, dear." She follows me into the kitchen. "Today went better than expected, huh?"

"I would say so. You know people say that the way you start your day reflects on how it will end."

"Oh, really," she says.

"That's right, and you know what?" I ask.

"What?"

"I may just have to agree with them because you started me off right today."

"Oh, really," she says again.

"After a round with you, I preach a great sermon, find the courage to invite the DuBoises over for dinner, take action to keep my job, and help unite Brayden with his father and Gloria with Terry. So, I would have to agree with them."

After I drop the dishes in the sink, she grabs my neck and spins me around. My lips soon encounter the softness of her lips that makes my knees shake. "Thank you."

"Thank you for what?" I ask.

"Thanks for not giving up on yourself," she says. "You made mistakes, but you kept trying; you didn't let go."

"Well, thank you, honey, but I should be thanking you. You are the one who gave me several chances."

"What can I say?" she asks. "I'm not glass; I'm the rock." She winks and returns her lips to mine. She stops abruptly. "You forgot about the rest of your matchmaking skills."

"What are you talking about, Rachel?"

"Did you forget Shaw and Brayden?"

After a short silence, we look at each other and laugh. "I guess you are right," I say, wrapping my arms around her. "Maybe I should start a matchmaking service."

Rachel moves so near I can smell her vanilla lip balm. "How about you start practicing your services right now."

CHAPTER 18: ERNEST LEE

Excerpts from Unlovable

∞ ∞ ∞

I was great and mighty. I was all things wonderful. I was perfect in every way. Then I lived. That life stalled my successes and scrambled my strength. Life surprised me with tears that followed smiles and screams that chased laughter like a rabid dog. My might was questioned, my greatness in doubt. I sit and wonder who can love me now.

When I thought I found love, love hadn't found me. Love was a distant and obscure mystery. In all of my days, I dare not say that love can be mastered, but it has surely mastered me. It drives me like a slave master. I need to love, need to be loved. It snaps my heart with a whip of loneliness in an attempt to keep me in my dark corner of isolation. It forces me to think, 'I'm not through with this corner yet. I still have trails for my tears to flow through. I still have more sorrow to sift. I still have more pain to process.' This darkness seems to be my friend. One day, I wake up in darkness, crying out in pain. I shout, 'Help me! Help me!' But, the darkness only taunts me, and that's when I realize darkness never loved me.

§§§§§

I awaken to darkness, and I write. I don't write because I want to or have been given some instruction to do so. I am merely writing because I can see. In fact, I feel I am one of the few left who actually see with their true eyes—the eyes of love. Many of us see through some lens of hatred, whether for self or others because there is something about us that is different. Far too often, difference is seen as deficiency. Our unique divinity is divided with demarcations, boxes, and bubbles, forcing us to split ourselves to "fit in" when we are an original design. Whatever stays inside the neat lines we create "fits in," and it is warmly received with our love. However, the original parts of us that won't be suppressed and dare to cross our self-constructed lines are seen as unlovable.

So, I cry each night, longing for a world that won't hate so much what it doesn't understand. It's as pointless as hating another planet because we don't know what's on it. It's like hating heat because we can't examine the sun's core. I cry, knowing that my brothers and sisters—of all colors, creeds, and compositions—and I lose control of fragments of our humanity when we are infected by the viral scourge of hate. Often, we are infected unaware, driven by its procreator, fear—and offspring—judgment and unforgiveness.

§§§§§

I sit here, attempting to dream with a broken heart. I imagine a brighter Earth. I dream of an alien race inspecting the Earth, and after they analyze the pyramids of Giza, the Great Wall of China and skyscrapers that litter cities across the globe, they will marvel at one monument above all else: The Statue of Liberty. It won't be the architectural design that will amaze them, but the symbol which the statue represents. With wars and rumors of wars, there is a poem that will startle and confound them. It is engraved on the tablet within the pedestal on which the statue stands. The poem is Emma Lazarus' "The New Colossus." She writes:

> Not like the brazen giant of Greek fame,
> With conquering limbs astride from land to land;
> Here at our sea-washed, sunset gates shall stand
> A mighty woman with a torch, whose flame
> Is the imprisoned lightning, and her name
> Mother of Exiles. From her beacon-hand Glows world-wide welcome; her mild
> eyes command
> The air-bridged harbor that twin cities frame.
> "Keep ancient lands, your storied pomp!" cries she
> With silent lips. "Give me your tired, your poor,
> Your huddled masses yearning to breathe free,
> The wretched refuse of your teeming shore.
> Send these, the homeless, tempest-tost to me,
> I lift my lamp beside the golden door!"

Now, I'm on a mission for love. As the Statue of Liberty is a symbol of hope and indiscriminate love, I desire to display a love that shines so bright the lost are found. I want my life's love to shine like a torch in the wilderness, guiding the tired, poor, and huddled masses into a promised land of love without end. Those who yearn to break away from the refuse of hatred's shore and breathe the air of freedom, they will find the nation of my heart pure and open to embracing their tempest-tossed souls.

I want to love the abused and scorned, lame and untamed. I want to love the homo, the hopeless, the hurt, and the heartless. The gangster, the thief, the killer, and the chief all are worthy of this love I long to share. I want to love what others throw away: the woman, the man, the in-between, the rich, the rapper, the slut, the saint, the bitter, the broken and diseased. God, help me to love what others throw away, even me. Help me to love all of me.

I'm on a mission to love because I know where love is you are. You are Love.

§§§§§

Everything has a limit, but love is just. It is as infinite as the Supreme God it represents. Love is present at all stages of existence. It can neither fail nor be defeated. The end of love is the end of God. Love can be suppressed but never conquered. That is why I continue to make the clarion call for someone to help me love the world. That is why I keep envisioning smiles on unfriendly faces and extended hands on clenched fists. Love can't fail.

Love is not just an action or feeling; it is an entity, a presence yearning for expression. Love is God, for God is love. We were created as a grand display of God's love, and the power inside of us stems from that love, a great love we must not fear. It can be intimidating to know we wield such great power; however, we will always fear others when we fear the greatness in ourselves. When that fear births hate, we will be fighting who we are more than the object of our hatred. We will be fighting the love, the essence of God, in us. Once we acknowledge and embrace the power of love inside of us, we will begin to overcome the obstacles that stand in the face of our own future.

So, I pray: Lord, help me to love above all else. Help me to love above all else.

§§§§§

UNLOVABLE

About the Author

Byron Jamal was adopted and raised in a loving home. With this shaping his perspective, he believes that love is the greatest power and gift we can possess. A suicide survivor and former pastor, Byron became the founder and CEO of The Call Path to fuse his expertise and unique perspective to empower everyday people and clients alike, including major corporations, public institutions, government agencies, and philanthropic organizations.

This dynamic writer is known for writing novels and plays comprised of real, practical, and savvy perspectives that bring out the best in people. As the author of the upcoming *Call Path* series, Byron Jamal guides his readers to discover their true purpose while maintaining a fulfilled life. Byron's use of wit and storytelling reveals the tools for achieving in every area of life and love—better relationships, positive habits, successful career goals, and healing from past challenges.

Byron received his Bachelor of Arts degree in English from Norfolk State University, an H.B.C.U., and earned a Master of Business Administration degree from Queens University of Charlotte. Before Queens University, Byron matriculated at Pittsburgh Theological Seminary under his mentor, Rev. Dr. Ronald E. Peters, where he gained immense respect for using theology to serve urban communities effectively. He became National Communications Chair for the National Urban League Young Professionals, supporting advocacy and aid efforts throughout the country, and continues to serve through motivational speaking, coaching, and philanthropy.

For more about Byron Jamal and his upcoming books and events, visit **www.byronjamal.com.**

I want to hear from you. Please leave a short review, thoughts, and reflections about this book on the platform you purchased it or send your comments to me in care of info@byronjamal.com.

Don't worry. No need to write an essay. Sharing a few sentences is brilliant.

Thank you in advance, PathFinder. Stay the Path.